Message to the Future

M. Jassma

No part of this publication may be reproduced in whole or in part, or stored in a retrieval system, or transmitted in any form or by any means, electronic, mechanical, photocopying, recording, or otherwise, without written permission of the author, except for the inclusion of brief quotations in a review.

Copyright © 2022 by M. Jassma
All rights reserved.

For information regarding permission, please write to:
info@barringerpublishing.com
Barringer Publishing, Naples, Florida
www.barringerpublishing.com

Design and layout by Linda S. Duider
Cape Coral, Florida

ISBN: 978-1-954396-16-6
Library of Congress Cataloging-in-Publication Data
Message to the Future / M. Jassma

Printed in U.S.A.

Message to the Future

DEDICATION

To my family, the ones who have lived with
me through this heartache and endured with
compassion and love.

I love you intensely and I'm honored we've travelled
this earthly journey together.

And

In memory of my son who I loved and to whom
I gave the best I had to give.

ACKNOWLEDGEMENTS

The editors who refined my work and helped offer this reflection on a section of my life.

Linda Duider of Barringer Publishing helped bring the imagined and rough images on the cover to life.

I am forever grateful to my mother, who through her human frailties, raised her children with care, understanding and love. She literally, in many ways, gave her life for us. She did the best she could with the resources she had. I endeavor everyday to honor her efforts.

My brother and confidant.

More broadly I acknowledge the many people who helped guide my life in a positive direction. Mr. Edward Charles Reilly who had a foundational impact when he gave me encouragement and instilled me with confidence to pursue higher educational goals. I'm additionally grateful to the teachers, on site administrators and nuns of Saint Mary's School who set examples of how to value each life and who tried to live in ways that showed us paths to what is right and good.

The priests, pastors, ministers, and preachers who offered

sermons of encouragement, promise and guidance that helped me see a positive path of existence in this world. In addition, I'm grateful for the Buddhist, Hindu, and Islamic writings that offered insight and perspective on a Creator who is too awesome to be called by one name. Even the negative message carriers showed me how I didn't want to exist in the world.

I'm grateful to J. Grieninger for that initial career boost and to the many others who believed in me. There are many who have influenced my life, sometimes through a kind word, encouragement, providing knowledge or opportunities. In the final analysis its difficult to capture the stitches that make up the tapestry of the person I've become.

Message to the Future

PREFACE

The little engine that could:
I think I can, I think, I can. I think I can. I know I can.

—Watty Piper

Life is full of twists and turns. We experience about every possible emotion before we finish our journey here on earth. I'm convinced the consistency of everyday living is a necessary foundation. That base is peppered with joyful events that keep us on balance when we encounter challenges.

It seems each of us was created with a particular Achilles heel that can upset our equilibrium. Sometimes, things happen that throw you so far off kilter, you wonder if you will ever make it back to your normalcy. On September 3, 1993, my life twisted into an unexpected rollercoaster ride of events and emotions. At times I still reel from the weight of it.

Until then, I led a pretty normal life. Having spent thirty-seven years experiencing living, I thought I had it figured out. My challenges were like those of many other modern day women. I had worked my way up in a large corporation where I was a contract negotiator. Although I was not formally performing duties as an attorney, I worked closely with them. I worked hard and performed well which made me professionally credible. My official workday ended at 5 p.m. However, there were frequent "unexpected" end of the day tasks. It seemed my boss would sit in his office and wait until 4 p.m. to identify crucial changes needed in a report which was to be released the next day. Those last minute tweaks often extended my work hours well beyond the anticipated departure time. That meant I had "homework."

Sometimes I had an assistant to help handle those spurious assignments, other times necessitated that I be on my own. Most of the personnel in my peer group were men, so I watched the "sport of the season" and memorized game scores to include myself in office conversations.

I enjoyed my career and sought to stay on top of my game by engaging in after-hours enrichment. Enriching my skills not only kept me well-informed in my current position, but also kept me postured for one I might seek in the event of an unexpected merger. So, I frequently read business articles at home and maintained connections with colleagues in other companies. Attaining the goals I set was a priority. In seeking professional utopia, I was aware that success has its costs. Clearly, I was willing to pay the cost in time and duty. My life was so full that I couldn't imagine anything other than my own physical illness taking it off course. It was unfathomable that my existing priorities would become meaningless.

That Friday started like most others. In the early morning, I walked into the garage to load Gabrielle's daycare needs into the car. I paused just for a moment at the edge of the garage thinking about Gabrielle's numerous ear infections. She was not yet two, but she had been to a doctor's office every three weeks or so for several months. We could not get her infections cleared up or understand what caused them. My department manager had absolutely no sympathy for my need to take her to the doctor.

My thoughts were interrupted by a wave of humid, Florida air. I instinctively raised my head and looked around the cul-de-sac. I surveyed seven neatly manicured lawns. A triumphant smile broke out on my face when I saw the grass in our yard was green and healthy. We had just re-sodded the lawn and installed a sprinkler system. Mike and I drove fifty miles each way to our jobs on Cape Canaveral. Mike was an executive with a different aerospace company; both our jobs were focused on safely launching the shuttle. Our work and commute had us away from home before sunrise until just before sunset, so we hired a lawn service to cut the grass. One of my joys was being outdoors, working in the yard and tackling the challenge of cultivating flowering plants in the Florida heat. Two retired neighbors in the cul-de-sac set the standard for lawn care, with impeccable looking green spaces, beautiful shrubs and healthy palm trees. The neatness and serenity of the neighborhood made me feel comfortable. I walked back into the house to finish the morning routine.

I yawned for the umpteenth time since getting up. Returning to work after Gabrielle's arrival left me feeling I never got enough sleep. We often had to get up before I could finish my best dreaming. When I heard her whine, I nudged Mike, "It's your turn."

He groggily yet dutifully got up and tended to her.

Mike and I had an agreement that we would take turns getting up with our child. Though Mike was really good about doing his part, when Gabrielle cried, I still woke up. If I went back to sleep, it was in intermittent dozes; I never felt rested. I can recall standing at the copy machine almost fully asleep before hearing someone ask, "You done?"

As a functioning zombie, my bleary-eyed existence was compounded that September morning because we were up late the night before talking to Justin. My seventeen-year-old son was enrolled in the local community college and trying to figure out his next steps in his journey through the world. Our primary focus was to encourage Justin to attend a seminar for teenagers. The organizers would discuss job opportunities. We thought he might find some interesting work he would enjoy doing. It was specifically targeted toward high-risk teenagers but we told him anyone could attend. My convincing tactics didn't seem effective so I enlisted Mike. Mike was good at persuasion, yet Justin remained uncommitted to the Saturday seminar.

Message to the Future

I paused at Justin's closed door on the way out of the house. I stood there thinking through my impulse to knock and let him know we were departing. I had long ago established the habit of knocking on his door to tell him I was leaving or had made it home. That day I suppressed the inclination because I thought, *since he's getting older, maybe he doesn't want me to do the things I've always done.* Justin's Friday class schedule didn't start until late afternoon. I had gotten three hours of coveted sleep last night and he had been up awfully late too. I decided not to bother him. I'd call him later after he had more uninterrupted sleep. But maybe my rationalizations were just a projection of my desires on him. In any case, I didn't knock. I turned from his door and headed to work. I left not knowing it would be the last day of the life I knew.

Part I

Part I

Message to the Future

CHAPTER ONE

Humpty Dumpty

> Humpty Dumpty sat on a wall
> Humpty Dumpty had a great fall.
> All the King's horses and all the king's men
> couldn't put Humpty together again.
>
> —Mother Goose

It was the beginning of a long, Labor Day weekend that I was more than ready for. Exhausted, I dropped into the passenger seat of our faithful, Honda Accord. We were proud of our eight-year-old, 1985 Honda Accord. We had dubbed it "The Green Pea." It had a manual transmission and the odometer registered 300,000 miles (more miles than the Space Shuttle had); it was still running strong. Glad to be done with the stresses of work, I turned to look at Gabrielle in the back seat; she was alternating between nonsensical chatter and toddler singing. She seemed stuck on "It's your birthday, it's your birthday, not for crisper, not for bisper, it's your birthday..."

Mike and I smiled at each other as we happily headed home. The sky was still blue and filled with puffy white clouds.

We had a new Camry in the garage, but because we accumulated so many miles during our daily commute, we opted to use our old Honda. When we needed to drive separately, Mike would drive the 1989 SEV6 king cab Nissan truck and I would drive the Honda. My son, Justin, had been living with his paternal grandparents but he was back with us now and he had the truck. We chose to drive on a quiet neighborhood street to avoid the stop and go traffic of Alafaya Trail. All of a sudden, The Green Pea made a little sigh then stopped. Turning the ignition again made it almost turn over but not quite; it went silent.

We had a state-of-the-art, Panasonic car phone. It was black and really heavy. It sat on a wide section of the floor and looked similar to an office desk phone except it plugged into the cigarette lighter. We used it to call AAA. The operator informed us, "It will be over an hour before anyone can call you back with a pickup time."

I asked, "Why? There is no adverse weather or excessive back up in this area."

"Ma'am, I can only tell you what the system is telling me."

"Thank you for your help."

I dropped the phone back into its cradle.

I complained to Mike, "What is the point of having a

service that's unavailable when you need it?"

He shrugged at me, sharing my resigned frustration. Entertaining Gabrielle in the car for more than an hour with just a few crackers was not the way I wanted to end my day. We thought a taxi might get us home. I dialed the operator and asked, "Would you give us the number of a taxi company?"

The operator questioned, "Which company?"

"We don't know, just any taxi company."

"You must ask for the taxi company by name because I am not allowed to give the telephone listing for any taxi company; it is considered unfair competition."

I explained, "We don't normally take taxis..."

I recalled seeing yellow taxis, so asked, "What is the number for The Yellow Taxi Company?"

"I'm sorry, there is no such local listing."

"Then would you please look up the first listing under the taxi heading?" After some haggling, she gave us a number, and the company was out of business. I handed the phone to Mike in frustration. He exasperatedly requested, "Close your eyes and pick one."

I could see we would be stranded in our car for a while. Clearly, freedom Friday was not evolving into a restful evening. I knew as the sun went down the mosquitoes would surely come out and if we had Gabrielle outside, they would unmercifully bite her delicate skin. I quickly tired of the ineffective results from phone calling and decided to walk home to get our other vehicle. I figured I could drive back to pick up Mike and Gabrielle before darkness descended.

I was a woman of action who wanted results. Mike was still pursuing taxi options when I mouthed, "I'm going to walk home and come back."

He acknowledged the plan by nodding and raising his hand. After walking several miles, I began to think I had been a little hasty in my decision. I began to realize it probably would take a couple of hours to reach my destination. Our home was at least ten miles from where our car had stopped. I covered the distance as quickly as I could in my navy blue pantsuit and two-and-a-half-inch high heels. I could see I had not walked fast enough because the sun was about to dip below the horizon. I could tell I had walked across the city line into our unincorporated area because the sidewalk came to an abrupt end and streetlights suddenly ceased to exist. It wasn't long before the sun dropped out of sight. The headlights of passing cars gave me some light as I continued to walk in the dark. A car drove up and stopped in front of me. I hoped it was not someone stopping to pester me because I was definitely not in the mood! I slowed my pace so that I could decide whether to stay in the grass, walk in the middle of the road, or just stay behind the car. If I could recall my college judo class, I could use my 116 pounds to flip a bigger person to the ground. I wished I had stuck with it; maybe it would have become second nature when danger was this close at hand. I slowed my pace as I kept my eye fixated on the familiar-looking car. A few minutes passed before Mike stuck his head out of the window and said, "It's me, honey."

I walked closer, opened the door, plopped in the seat and asked, "How did you beat me home?"

"I was eventually able to get a taxi, picked up our car and came looking for you."

I was relieved to see him because I was really worn out. I obviously needed more endurance training. Mike headed home. I had covered a good distance; we were within a mile of our subdivision entrance. Mike said in a somber voice, "Honey, Justin has done something to himself."

I immediately thought, *I sure hope he didn't take too much of that stomach medication.*

I turned my head to respond. When I looked at Mike, I saw his eyes were bigger than I'd ever seen them. Mike solemnly said, "He committed suicide."

At that moment everything went black. I was still conscious but my being began to sink into a wide, deep hole. I could hear my hoarse voice somewhere out there crying "NOOOOOOOOOOOO ... My baby, not my baby!" I sobbed as I slid from my seat toward the floor and got into a little ball. My mind opened to blank space and my entire body was numb. Through that distant hollowed out space, I heard my sobbing. I could feel myself sinking farther and farther into that dark hole. Mike stopped the car and gently pulled me up from the little ball I had gotten into between the seat and dashboard. He got back in the car. When I looked up, I saw we had driven past our subdivision. Maybe the police had taken Justin's body somewhere and Mike was taking me to him, but he stopped at a gas station and went inside. He stayed in there. I wondered, *what is he doing? Why isn't he going home or to the police or wherever Justin is?* I got out of the car and started walking home, but Mike stopped me saying "Come back to the car."

In a weak but determined voice I said, "I want to see him."

Then Mike's quandary surfaced.

"The police told me to stay away from our home and not to bring you around Justin's body."

My flashing eyes conveyed how asinine that sounded to me. I didn't say anything. In a compassionate tone Mike murmured, "We'll go home."

Our house was on a half-acre lot and was situated at twelve o'clock on the cul-de-sac. I could see the tree-line behind our house. Our neighborhood was usually very quiet and dark at that time of the evening. It was shocking to see red and yellow flashing lights pervertedly disco-swirling from the top of the big, red, fire truck. The lights and radio communication from the police cars parked at the driveway announced their presence in front of our home. I wanted to get out and run into his bedroom to see him. I didn't realize he wasn't in his bedroom.

As if in a hazy dream, I slowly tiny-stepped my way toward our home. A man stood in front of me blocking my progress at the driveway; his demanding voice and outstretched arms halted all motion.

He barked, "You can't come here."

There was 100 feet of driveway from the cul-de-sac to the house. I looked up the driveway past the crepe myrtle trees, past the magnolia tree and saw a covered heap on the ground. Someone, I believe it was the man who stopped me, took me to the fire truck and instructed me to sit on a bench just inside the door. The door was in the middle of the truck. I sat on the bench. Directly across from the bench was an axe. I looked at the equipment, the oxygen tanks, hoses, face masks and then my eyes returned to the axe. I thought about chopping my foot with the axe, then I thought of splitting my head open. But I didn't move. I sat there frozen, gazing at the axe. Then—for some strange, unknown reason—laughter burst out in my head. I wanted to give myself over to the relief of laughter; I restrained myself because I knew it was illogical. I squashed the laughter in my head, putting a net around it and pulling the ends tighter and tighter until the laughter was pea sized. I sat there in a frozen position holding my pea-sized laughter under control. I believed freedom was available to me if I opened up to laughter, but something inside me knew that I would enter a new world from which I would never return. I had to decide if I wanted to go there. At that moment, a fireman came into the truck and said, "You have to leave."

I was reluctant because I thought if I moved the net

would be released and either I would laugh hysterically or flail about and wail in utter despair. I rose shakily and walked down the two, deep, rubber-coated steps to the black asphalt. I felt as if I was stepping into an unfamiliar world. Mike was waiting at the bottom of the last step and when he reached for my arm; his touch helped me to stay grounded.

I turned and stood looking up the driveway at the covered pile on the ground. I did not want to believe Justin had died. He was over six feet four inches. How could he be in such a tiny heap on the ground? Why had they put him on the ground? Mike interrupted my thoughts when he said, "Let's go sit in the car. The investigators just warned me again that we had to stay at least 100 feet away. It is a rule or law or something."

I asked, "Are they in his room bothering his stuff?"

Mike responded, "I was told they had not been in there yet. They're concentrating on the garage and the driveway."

It didn't occur to me to ask why.

We sat in the car for some time. There was a streetlight at the entrance to the cul-de-sac. It shed enough light to see the darkened trees, grass and sky; strangely even though the houses were there amidst everything, somehow my vision only took in nature. The county investigator finally came over and explained, "We have to conduct a thorough investigation. It will take some time, but we want to be thorough. I will come back and talk with you about everything. I think your wife should see your son's body later. It might be too much for her right now. I believe you should leave and return when we have completed our investigation."

I heard myself insipidly say, "I am not leaving."

The investigator looked at me for a few moments as if he was about to say something, but he turned and went back into the house.

Mike and I sat in the car and waited. My thoughts began to wander. Feeling the need for fresh air, I pushed myself up out of the car and stood letting the gentle, night breeze brush against my cheeks. I looked up at the stars, closed my eyes and whispered a request, "I just want someone to pray over his body."

As the words left my lips, I opened my eyes to see Mike and Pastor Tim standing near me. I had not seen or heard his car arrive. Tears flooded my eyes because I felt a prayer was being answered. I closed my eyes to pray with Pastor Tim. When I looked up again, I saw my sister-in-law, Cynthia and her husband, Bobby Royel.

Cynthia rubbed my neck as we sat in the car waiting for them to pray over his body. Suddenly, I bolted upright and said, "They laid Justin's body on the hard, dirty ground and the Florida bugs are going to get on him!"

Gary, Pastor Tim and Bobby heard me as they were walking back. Pastor Tim assured me, "No, no, it's alright. There is some material on the ground beneath his body and a different piece of material is covering his body."

I could hear my sounds of anxiety settle down.

Message to the Future

CHAPTER TWO

Rock-A-Bye Baby

Rock a bye baby, on the tree top,
When the wind blows the cradle will rock.
When the bough breaks the cradle will fall,
And down will come baby, cradle and all.

Rock a bye baby, gently you swing,
Over the cradle, Mother will sing,
Sweet is the lullaby over your nest
That tenderly sings my baby to rest.

From the high rooftops, down to the sea
No one's as dear as baby to me
Wee little hands, eyes shiny and bright
Now sound asleep until morning light

Rock a bye baby, on the tree top,
When the wind blows the cradle will rock.
When the bough breaks the cradle will fall,
And down will come baby, cradle and all.

—Mother Goose

I recalled my last conversation with Justin.

I hadn't been in my office long; Justin called at eight thirty. I was surprised he had gotten up so early.

"Where should I take this check?"

I reluctantly responded, "I don't know where the warehouse is located. I know the directions don't make sense so Mike will call about ten with clearer directions."

Agitated, Justin asked, "What is it for?"

Exasperated, I replied, "It's just an order, Mike will give you the details. Put the truck key on your key ring so you don't lose it."

"Okay. But I heard you laughing about me, saying that I was going to kill myself."

In an incredulous tone, "Justin you are wrong!!"

I couldn't believe he thought I would laugh at something like that. I didn't hear you say anything like that!!! Then I thought, *maybe he is trying to manipulate me by making me feel sorry for him.*

Matter-of-factly I said, "Everything we talk about is not about you. We did not laugh about you! We were not laughing at you. What made you think we were laughing at you?"

He responded, "I heard you say, 'Justin was talking about killing himself and start laughing.'"

I thought about telling him our conversation was only about him going to the seminar, but I remembered someone in the family said he was a panderer. I loved him and never saw or thought anything like that. But on the spur of the moment I thought, *I can't let him try to control me this way.*

So instead, I said, "That is very wrong. Before you returned, we talked about other things and we still talk about other things. We were not laughing at you!"

He asked, "Do you know the directions to this place?"

"No, I don't know them."

"Where is the place? What part of town?"

I unfortunately had not learned areas outside our immediate area.

Exasperated, I said, "I don't know."

He paused. Then asked, "Do you have Darlene's number?"

"I think I do, but I don't have it with me."

"Well, I will at least leave that for you."

"Okay."

He gave me the telephone number then said, "I love you Mom."

"I love you too."

I looked up and my boss was in the doorway telling me there was an important meeting we had to attend. He stood there waiting for me. I interrupted Justin, "I'll call you back."

We hung up.

I sat in the meeting wondering what Justin was about to say. I can't recall a word of the important meeting. I escaped from the meeting about nine o'clock and called Justin but couldn't reach him. I let the phone ring a long, long time, but there was no answer. My first impulse, or really a feeling inside said: go home.

I rationalized that away, reached for the phone and dialed Justin again. No answer.

My eye caught the movement of an investigator as he left the driveway and returned to the garage. The only humans left outdoors were Mike, me and the investigators.

We waited, waited and waited. I called Ms. Lyonns and numbly said, "Justin won't be paying back the money; he's dead." Sounding as if she couldn't believe what she heard Ms. Lyonns asked, "What?"

In a bland voice I told her, "Justin committed suicide."

She sounded hurt and was crying as she strained to tell Mr. Lyonns, "Don, Justin killed himself."

Then she returned her attention to me, "Justin told John he felt so bad he could kill himself."

I made another call. The dial tones of the car phone cut through the silence like a megaphone, then vibrated in the air.

"Mike turn down the volume."

He looked around the phone, "I don't know how."

Mother's answering machine was on. She was probably still at the hospital. She worked long, hard hours as a nurse; she always had. I dropped the phone into its cradle in disappointment. I was too worn out and frustrated to continue but I thought I should tell someone in my family before the news spread through our small town. I didn't want my mother surprised with a news bulletin from some uncaring gossiper. Mike called my sister, GiGi. I heard her gasp "Oh no!!" when Mike told her what happened. I was confident she would spread the word to Mother, and many others.

A few moments later, the chief investigator walked over and concluded his investigation by saying, "I'm taking some letters that belonged to your son. I promise to return them to you when I'm done."

I looked up and a lady I'd never seen stood beside the investigator. He introduced her. "This is Jeannie. She is from the victim's advocate office."

Jeannie took a small step forward, "I'm sorry about your son. Is there anything I can do?"

I hung my head and slowly shook it's heavy weight as I responded, "No."

She looked around and replied, "It looks like you have lots of support. Please call me if there is any way I can help."

She gently slipped her card into my hand.

The chief investigator spoke again instructing, "Sleep somewhere else tonight. The house is full of carbon monoxide. It could kill you while you sleep."

That night, Mrs. Lamm solemnly welcomed us into her home. Before falling asleep I told Mike, "I want to go to Tallahassee to see Darlene early in the morning while the sun is shining brightly."

CHAPTER THREE

Boy and Girl

> There was a little boy and a little girl
> Lived in an alley:
> Says the little boy to the little girl,
> "Shall I, oh, shall I?"
> Says the little girl to the little boy,
> "What shall we do?"
> Says the little boy to the little girl,
> "I will kiss you."
>
> —Mother Goose

Mike and I met in 1985. We both worked for an aerospace company on Long Island. I had been there over a year when a colleague came by my desk.

"I've got someone for you to meet."

"Who?"

"He's a new guy here. His office is in the building across the street. A buddy I used to work with knows him well."

He winked at me, "He's got a good job."

Mike was a tall, eye-catching, 6'4", 210 pound man who

wore well-made suits and shirts with his initials on the sleeves. He was a smart, charming, well-mannered guy.

My sister, Angela, was living with Justin and me and so I thought he was the perfect fit for her. When Justin was visiting his dad, Angela, Mike and I had fun exploring New York City on the weekends. But my plans for them were not their plans.

Angela observed, "He's the kind of guy you need in your life. He's conscientious and courteous and he likes you. He'll be good for you."

"I don't know; he might be too boring."

"Maybe you need boring these days."

That was her take; I loved Angela and knew she had a good head and observational skills. That made it easier to see him in a different light. But after the catastrophe of my first marriage to John, I wasn't jumping into a serious relationship so fast. We continued to do all of our socializing together. It would be a while before we became a true couple.

CHAPTER FOUR

I See the Moon

I see the moon
The moon sees me
The moon sees somebody I'd like to see
God Bless the moon
God Bless me
God Bless the somebody I'd like to see

—Mother Goose

Life changed for us when Angela became gravely ill that summer. When we could, we ate dinner together during the week but always on the weekends. One evening at dinner, she started relating how something was wrong, "I feel tired all the time. My arms ache and I can hardly walk up the subway stairs."

I asked, "Are there a lot of them?"

"I count them every day. There are twenty-two on one platform and twenty-four on another."

"Does anybody bother you or knock into you?"

"Nobody bothers me and I try to stay out of the way."

I was concerned yet admired her for handling the hustle and bustle of Manhattan. I looked at her naturally thin body, weighing no more than 105 pounds, her light brown hair hung down her back but I noticed her arms were sticks, with no muscle tone. She coughed. It was so soft I thought she was attempting to be dainty. We mulled it over and thought she was overworked. We attributed the tired feeling to the long hours of work and the commute. We decided it was draining both mentally and physically. She tried vitamins, something the doctor prescribed, and a healthier diet, adding more salads with no results. After brainstorming sessions, we brilliantly determined a little relaxation would help. Angela had always dreamed of seeing Paris so we booked our flights to Europe. Justin opted to visit with his dad in Toledo.

Youthful optimism had us hope and believe the unbelievable. Her condition continued to deteriorate. The doctor's thought Angela had some kind of contagious disease. Specialists in white lab coats with masks flooded her hospital room. I had to wear a gown, cap, mask and gloves when I visited. After a battery of tests, one wise doctor did a biopsy of the muscle tissue in her thigh—he found it! I telephoned Angela from the road while on a business trip. Her first excited words were, "You don't have to put on all that protective gear anymore!"

"Why, what did they find?"

"It's polymyositis."

Not only was her body attacking her muscles, she had schleraderma which caused her skin to harden and Reynaud's Syndrome, which had her unable to tolerate cold, not even ice cream. Our glee was fleeting as the nuances of the diseases unfolded. The treatments were experimental at best. There was no cure.

We resolved she had to return to Toledo to get the daily care she needed. She went home to a hospital system and doctors my mother knew. I applied for jobs in the area and landed one in Cincinnati, Ohio. I was at least within reasonable driving distance. Justin happily went to spend time with his father, until I could get settled in a new location. Mike and I continued to date. Even when we decided to officially date, I didn't invite him to meet my son.

I was a little surprised when he asked, "When am I going to meet your son?"

"I don't think that will happen for a while."

"Why is that?"

"I don't want a bunch of men in and out of my child's life. I can date you without you meeting him. That way if anything happens between us it won't affect him."

"We're dating exclusively. Nothing is going to happen between us."

When I visited Mike and his family, I watched him with

is nieces and nephews, with his sisters and brothers, with his parents and friends. He seemed to be a loving, caring person in every case. They all seemed to love and respect him. He seemed like a truly, good guy but we had that conversation a few times before I invited him to Ohio to meet Justin. Soon after, Mike's job brought him to Ohio on a regular basis.

I found a townhome north of Cincinnati. Justin rejoined me; then, as Angela got better, she joined us. In those days, I would sit in a chair near Justin's bed and read to him at night in my eternal effort to get him to read more. One of those nights Justin shared, "I have this energy inside me mom that just keeps going."

I didn't know what that meant. He had stopped playing basketball when we left New York. I thought maybe he needed another sport, so with much convincing he began football. Football allowed him to become connected with a particular group at school. He played one year then moved on to baseball; the sport he actually loved. That resulted in a different friend group and a lot of time spent in batting cages. I wasn't sure if I should encourage more sports ... he needed to keep his grades up. I decided more sports wasn't a good option. In an effort to teach him responsibility and have him earn a little spending money, I encouraged a few hours of weekend busboy duty at Perkins. I didn't know what he meant by energy inside him. He was young, maybe all boys had that energy.

Justin was a fun loving teen. I enjoyed listening to the music he liked. It was mostly New Edition, Whitney Houston,

The Beach Boys, and other upbeat songs. Typically, in the store, he would urgently say some version of, "Mom, mom, look, look over there!"

I'd turn to look and he would grin, "That mannequin is smiling at you."

"Boy, stop being so silly!"

He would laugh his head off.

I introduced Mike to Justin. They seemed to bond. We all went out to eat when he was in town. The fad was to shave words in hairstyles; Mike used clippers to cut Justin's name in his hair. Mike also went to Justin's football games when he was in town. Sometimes, all four of us went into the basement to dance. Chuckling, Justin said, "Mom you dance like this."

He would sway from side to side with a goofy look on his face. I'd laugh and say, "Funny, Justin, I know I dance better than that."

"Mike dances like an old man. This is how he moves on every record."

He would hunch his shoulders and do a little tight step moving each foot in then out. Mike would say, "You are just a funny guy, Justin, how do you dance?"

Smoothly responding with that fun-filled, mischievous, Justin grin, "Can't tell you. It's a secret."

Angela just smiled at us. She was his buddy; he never made fun of her.

Our lives were good for a while. Mike and I spent a lot of time together despite the miles between us. Everyone seemed happy. Gradually, Angela spent more time in the basement because it was really warm there with the fireplace on. I don't know when it happened but one day she got dressed for work, but said she couldn't do it. She couldn't go anymore.

"Don't worry about it. Just stay home until you feel better. I'll call your job and tell them you're ill."

January 1987, Angela got pneumonia. Mother visited us in Ohio to nurse her back to health. She seemed to get better but two weeks after Mother left, she got really cold and I had to take her to the hospital. Mother returned to Ohio. Angela's face remained swollen from the steroids but we watched her once fit body deteriorate. I'm not sure but I think it all happened in a two week span. One morning, the hospital called shortly after I arrived at work. Someone from the hospital said, "Come right away she is going to have an operation on her heart." I was able to see her before she went into the operating room. The tubes were everywhere. She had one stuck down her throat so she couldn't speak. I held her hand and looked deep into her eyes. Her eyes were bigger and brighter than I had ever seen them. Our hearts seemed to touch at that moment. I said, "Fight, be strong and fight."

Mother and I sat outside the operating room for a long time then we went to a private waiting room. Somehow,

Justin was in the private waiting room when we walked in. I jumped when I heard the loud splat. I turned around and saw Justin had smacked the hospital wall really hard when the doctor told us Angela had died. I thought he might have hurt himself. I knew he was disappointed, he had opted not to go to the hospital the night before and he was so upset that he had lost that last chance to see her. I understood. I had been exhausted and said I had to make sure Justin studied for a test. She said, "Go, he needs that support." My mother wanted to visit with my aunt. No one was there when her life was in peril.

Angela and I always had a strong relationship. I had been ecstatic to have a sister when she was born and over the years, she became my best friend. She had been the one to baby-sit Justin while I worked and finished my degree at the local college. After she graduated from college, she lived with us. I was so numb, I'm not sure I was much help to Justin. I mustered, "Stop, I don't want you to break anything." I eventually rose from my seat to embrace him and try to calm him, but we both lost an irreplaceable friend. He had lost his aunt and surrogate mother. She had been an integral part of our lives. February 26, 1987, my beloved sister took her last breath on this earth, but the loss would be felt for years to come.

The wind whipped around us as Justin and I stood together looking into the grave. Others had long ago sought the shelter of their cars. Some left, some watched as we sadly stood on that cold, February day; it was a long time before we returned to that black limousine.

It was serendipitous that Mother and GiGi argued and GiGi moved in with us in March. I couldn't tell that she was pregnant but at her eighth month, she became ill. That prompted a big discussion about pre-natal care, insurance, delivery, etc. In July, she decided to return home. Justin and I were alone again.

A big quiet spot had opened up after Angela's death; it could not be filled with the noise of life. Maybe I would be next? I wrote Justin this note and filed it in my Bible.

> Justin, I love you very, very much.
> More than words can say.
> Try to be good and be the best you can be.
> Even when I'm not here, I am with you.
> Make me proud, but more importantly
> make yourself proud. Stay away from what
> is bad. God will give you strength if you
> have faith. If you surround yourself with
> good people who try to do good things, you
> will be fine. Choose your friends carefully.
> There is no excuse—no drugs of any kind
> (you know what I mean). Let Mike and
> Mother guide you. I want the very best for you

in life, but YOU make your life whatever it is.

Love Always and Forever
Mom 6/29/88

I could not have known, five years later I would need to take my own advice.

Not long after Angela's death the principal of his junior high school called me for a meeting.

The principal sternly stated, "Justin was caught with a pocketknife. That is against the rules. He will be suspended from school for three days."

I asked, "May I see the knife?"

It was small.

I asked, "Justin is this yours?"

"Yes."

I asked, "Why do you have it?"

"I just have it in case."

"In case of what?"

"Anything."

I was deflated. The principal excused Justin.

We spoke at length. I told him, "I think Justin feels some of the boys might gang up on him because he stood up for a Jewish boy they were picking on."

It didn't matter. Rules were rules.

Teary eyed I told him, "It's been hard for Justin, he just lost his aunt who was very important in his life and it's a period of adjustment for him."

I tried to maintain my dignity and remain professional but I could not stop those big water drops from flowing as I spoke. He was silent for a few minutes then assessed, "It sounds like you both have some adjustments.

I will give him an in school suspension for three days. He will go to study hall."

Not knowing anything else appropriate to say, I thanked him and left.

I was glad it was his last year at Hopewell junior high. Not just because of this incident but because his favorite teacher had told him he shouldn't be working at the Perkins restaurant; he was too young. He was fifteen. I was trying to teach him responsibility. It was the first time I began to wonder if trying to put him in the best schools had made him a target—simply because he stood out—drew attention for looking different from the rest. Anything, large or small, was a major infraction waiting to be addressed.

Message to the Future

CHAPTER FIVE

A Wish

> I would like to be a queen,
> And walk in gardens green,
> And to have the pages all before me bow.
> And I ever would be seen
> Guarded by the soldiers keen,
> With a gleaming golden crown upon my brow
>
> —Mother Goose

March 1989, Mike and I were engaged, with a late, June 1990 wedding date. Justin and I talked it over. I assumed he liked Mike. They got along. When Mike called and I was too tired to speak with him, Justin asked in a concerned voice, "What's wrong? You don't like him anymore?

"Yes, I like him but I'm exhausted."

So, I was surprised when he started a discussion by saying, "I don't want you to get married."

"Why?"

He gave me a typical teenage cryptic reply, "I just don't."

"Does Mike treat you funny or badly when I'm not around?"

"No."

"Does he look at you in a weird way when I'm not looking?"

"No."

"Has he ever said or done anything bad to you?"

"No."

"Why don't you want me to marry him?"

"I just don't."

"Your dad has a girlfriend and two children and you seem fine with that."

"That's different."

"How?"

"It's just different."

"Unless you give me a reason not to marry Mike, I'm going to do it."

He didn't say anything.

So, I bolstered my position, "No matter what, I will always love you. It will be a better life for us."

Justin called his dad, then later reported to me, "Dad is surprised you're getting married. He thought you would remarry him and we would all be back together again."

"I'm surprised at that!"

A few days later he started the conversation again, "Dad is thinking about getting married."

"That's good."

"He won't get married if I tell him not to."

"How can you say that? He's a grown man. He'll do what he wants to do."

"We have that kind of relationship. He won't marry if I tell him not to."

"Don't you want your brother and sister to have him with them while they are growing up? Help them with homework and tuck them in bed at night?"

Sadly, Justin responded, "He can still be with them..."

We left that conversation hanging in the air. I could only see the potential good; I wanted him to see it too.

I thought things would settle down; we would move away and start a new happy life. But before that could happen, late in 1989, real trouble started. I sat in my office working, answered the phone, and was surprised to hear a police officer from Lakota high school. He assured, "Your son is okay but there has been an incident that we need to discuss with you."

I left work and met the officers in a little, unkempt, storage room at the school. One of the officers picked up a phone on a little table and had someone call Justin from class.

When he arrived, one officer spoke to me but looked at Justin and accused, "Justin destroyed a semi-truck at a company not far from your home."

I asked, "Justin did you do it?"

"No."

I questioned the officers, "When did the incident occur and why are you so sure Justin was involved?"

They gave me a date and I recalled Justin was with his friend, Roy, on that date. They replied, "Roy has been implicated too."

I inquired, "By whom?"

According to the officers, "We've been working with a juvenile who has been in trouble with the law on several occasions. He was a witness and turned them in."

I queried, "What makes him credible?"

The main officer asserted, "We have successfully tried a number of cases based on his testimony and we have confidence in him."

I wondered out loud, "Have fingerprints been taken?"

The officer stated, "There were too many prints on the truck for the process to be meaningful."

I insisted, "I'll pay for it."

The officer smugly replied, "It wouldn't mean anything."

The stress of the situation let silent tears escape my eyes. I thought about how I had tried to make sure Justin lived in a good environment and how I had tried to protect him from crime and other pitfalls of life. Justin looked on.

One of the officers turned to Justin, "You can return to class."

When he left, the main officer informed me with conviction, "We will not drop our pursuit. We will be getting in touch with you soon."

That night Justin and I discussed the officers' accusations. I questioned, "Are you sure you didn't do anything wrong?"

"I'm sure. They tried to do the same thing to Josh, but Josh's parents hired a high-powered attorney who told the police to leave them alone. "

I told him, "We don't know an attorney like that and I hope you are innocent so we don't need an attorney."

Almost sympathetically, "Don't worry Mom; it'll be alright."

I could hear Justin telling me, "You're too serious Mom. It's my job to make you laugh."

I love tapped him, "No it's not. Your job is to be a good person and a good student."

I just wasn't comfortable with the situation. I needed a sanity check. Mike and I had been engaged for a year and I was embarrassed and hesitant to disclose this latest problem, but this was part of my life and he needed to know these details. Mike was concerned but said, "I don't believe the charges and 'proof' would stand up in court."

I was still concerned that the police targeted him. I was aware some youngsters like Justin, guilty or not, had their lives destroyed when police decided they were guilty. I was grateful there was only a month left in the school year and we would be leaving Ohio to start anew in Florida.

CHAPTER SIX

A Cock and Bull Story

> The cock's on the house-top blowing his horn;
> The bull's in the barn a-threshing of corn;
> The maids in the meadows are making of hay;
> The ducks in the river are swimming away.
>
> —Mother Goose

We moved to Florida and wed within the week. Final preparations were hectic but Justin seemed supportive. I had planned to take Justin with us on our honeymoon. Mike wasn't keen on that idea. Justin wanted to go to California to visit Sheila, a family friend who knew John well. I told him I'd made arrangements for him to stay with Mrs. Lamm until we returned; it was only one week. He begged and pleaded for a long time and finally came up with a reason I should let him go. He promised to attend summer school. I caved. We all went to the airport together, but our flight left first so I kissed him on the cheek, made him promise to call and we left for the Caribbean. A few minutes later, Mrs. Lamm put Justin on a plane to California.

We spoke often during his time in California and he complained about what I thought were little things, mostly rules. Sheila said she insisted they come right home after school. A month later, when summer school was over, I coordinated with Sheila to ensure he got to the airport on time. I anxiously waited at the Orlando airport for Justin's flight. I waited and waited for him to disembark. They closed the door, the anxious smile fell off my face and my heart dropped to my stomach. I frenetically checked at the counter. "Are you sure everyone is off the plane?"

"Yes, they're cleaning it now."

"My son. My son was on this flight, but he didn't get off."

The agent said, "Yes, I believe he was on the plane, but he got off before we departed from California."

I was desperate. I went to the pay phone to call Sheila. In a low, solemn voice, "Justin wasn't on the plane."

She responded, "He was acting funny, distant and cold, so I left after I put him on the plane."

I didn't believe Justin would get off the plane on his own. He was not an audacious child. He had to be with someone he knew! My mind was somewhere between an emotional black pit and uncontrolled energy when I inserted more coins to call Mike at work. He told me to call the police.

I had created this. I had made the bad decision to let him go to California. But I had to focus; I wanted to find my child. I spent my energy looking for information. I called my mother seeking support. She too recommended alerting the police. I called the police department in Toledo. The feeling reminded me of the time we had split up and John took Justin from the daycare. I frantically searched everywhere but John didn't bring him back until very late at night. As I had back then, I called the Lyonnses looking for John. The Lyonnses were a large, close-knit family of beautiful exotic-looking people. They behaved as if their family was the center of the universe and only sanctioned outsiders mattered. The matriarch, Mrs. Lyonns, often let Mr. Lyonns take front and center but everyone knew where to go for coordination or answers. The family members often visited the homestead. John's older brother, Karl, answered the phone and said, "I've got a friend in the police department. He used to be one of my fraternity brothers."

I knew Karl to be crafty like a politician, but at the time I just wanted help from anyone. He gave me his friend's phone number, "Give him a call he will help you." It turns out Mr. Mann was an investigator on the police force. I explained the situation and he said, "I'll look into it. Call me anytime."

I then called the Orange County, California, Sheriff's Office and the police department. I called everyone I could think of. I called one of my friends who had a brother on the Toledo police force. I spoke to her mother telling her the story. In her dismay she exclaimed "Lord have mercy." I called everyone I knew in Toledo. I began to think of anyplace I knew

John had been. I called all the law enforcement departments of those places; police departments in Gary, Indiana; Los Angeles, California; Chicago, Illinois; Hattiesburg, Mississippi; New Orleans, Louisiana; Knoxville, Tennessee police and their county and sheriff departments. Some of the officers asked, "Why don't you want your son with his father?"

"Because he is a drug dealer."

"How do you know?"

"I just know."

I thought they were supposed to be a source of help. Maybe something prevented them from offering assistance, but none showed any interest in ever telling me what I might do to find my son.

Finally, I called the National Missing Children Bureau and got a case number. Days later, I circled back to Sheila. She told me her sister had been visiting and saw Abbie, John's sister-in-law, in a park. Reportedly, her sister explained I was looking for Justin. According to her, Abbie snappily replied, "What happens between Mary Lou and John is their business."

It was hearsay, but still, the few times I had spent with Abbie had me think she was more sensitive. I couldn't dwell on that. Since John's brother, Kerry, and his wife, Abbie, were coincidentally in California, I suspected they knew where Justin was. I suspected John was involved. It was starting to appear the Lyonnses knew where he was but no one was willing to help me.

After more than a week of telephone searching, I told Mike, "I'm going to California to find him."

Mike asked, "Where would you start?"

"Where he was last seen."

"You've already asked Sheila everything. What more can you find out if you're there?"

"I don't know, but I have to try."

I didn't go because Mr. Mann kept promising, "I'm on the verge of getting your son back to you."

Then, Karl Lyons called, "I contacted John and found out Justin is with him. I'm trying to persuade John to send Justin home."

"Where are they?"

He paused for a minute then replied, "I can't tell you that."

I called Mr. Mann relaying all to him. He repeated, "I'm on the verge of getting your son back to you."

That's when I knew. The Lyonnses knew and, as always, stuck together whether they were right or wrong. From experience, I knew I couldn't believe anything they would say. Mr. Mann was in on it too, keeping me from speaking to a true police official who actually might have helped me. He was a dishonest policeman and an immoral human. I was unsure of Sheila's role in this but only ugly hearts could have conducted and kept up such a wicked charade.

I phoned my mother again as I did several times a day. She told me, "I saw Justin with John! I tried to talk to John but he went to the trunk of his car as if he was going to get a gun. I drove off."

"That was the wisest thing to do. I wouldn't want you to get hurt."

Justin came home at the end of August and was late starting school.

When he got off the plane I said, "I've been worried about you. You know you shouldn't have gone anywhere without my knowledge. Where were you?"

He wouldn't say. I had never denied John access to Justin so I couldn't understand why he would kidnap him. I couldn't get answers to any of my questions, from my child or from any adults. I decided to put it behind me and try to move toward a more positive life. In hindsight, I wish I had filed an official police report that exposed all of their unscrupulous behaviors.

Message to the Future

CHAPTER SEVEN

A Tisket, A Tasket

> A tisket, a tasket, A green and yellow basket,
> I wrote a letter to my love, And on the way I dropped it.
> I dropped it, I dropped it, And on the way I dropped it.
> A little boy picked it up And put it in his pocket.
>
> —Mother Goose

I remained hopeful we could start our new family life and Justin would flourish with a fresh start, leaving the Ohio troubles behind. About a month or so after residing in Orlando, a letter from the Ohio sheriff arrived. I ignored it and tried to create normalcy.

I was happy to welcome Justin's first, new school friend, Kevin, for a sleepover. I began to have a clear awareness of Justin's actions during Kevin's visit. We ordered pizza and I put ten dollars of change on a table in our bedroom; it was missing. Later that evening, when Justin went to the bathroom, I casually questioned his friend who told me Justin had briefly gone into our bedroom while I was gathering their food. It wasn't a mistaken misplacement; Justin had stolen that money.

I started reflecting on why Justin would steal. While there were other family influences, John and I were the ones he looked up to the most. I know he knew it was wrong. The reason for stealing had to be something we were doing or not doing to have him behave this way.

To a girl who spent formative years in Catholic school and churches, John had seemed like a good guy. He used to help old ladies cross the street with their groceries, was beyond loyal to his family and valued little children by playing games with them. Yet, he kidnapped my child. While trying to take the high road, I remained uneasy with him and what he did. Very surprisingly, John had the audacity to call one October day to say he and his buddies would be riding through the area on the way to New Orleans and wanted to stop by to see Justin. Justin was beyond excited that his dad would be visiting him. Mike reluctantly agreed John could come to our home.

The guard had called to let us know they were on the way. They knocked; I opened the door to John and two others. They sat. I offered them glasses of water. I sat across the room uneasily watching them. A sweaty glass of ice water sat on the black end table, two more sat on the coffee table. Each was slowly dripping onto round, leather coasters. Two of the visitors were seated on the mauve, leather sofa facing the entertainment unit. John sat with his legs crossed at the knee in a stuffed, leather chair of the same color. His high-buffed caramel shoe looked like a trophy on the light grey carpet. John's back was to the patio door and Justin stood slightly behind his chair hovering over his dad like he was a prized possession. My son had a pleasant smile on his face and every few minutes, it spontaneously broke into a grin.

The chair John chose afforded him a view of the entire condo. To his left was the hallway leading to the main bathroom, second bedroom and master bedroom suite. In front of him was the dining area, with a black lacquered dining room table and matching chairs. The cushions on the chairs were covered in a grey fabric to match the walls. To the left of that Mike stood, barely visible, behind the counter in the small kitchen. Mike busied himself cleaning the grates from the stove. I could feel his tension. I had pulled out a chair from the dining table and turned it around to sit facing them. My back was erect with sandaled feet planted firmly on the floor.

There was a lot of chatter about little or nothing.

The air conditioner clicked on again and provided a familiar hum. The room felt too small. I looked to my right across the kitchen counter, Mike continued to work on something in the kitchen but I could tell he was listening intently. I got up to refill my glass with water.

John finally spoke up, "I want to spend a little time with Justin. I'll take him out to eat and bring him back."

"John, I'm not sure I can trust you to get him back on time."

"You can trust me. I promise I will get him back this evening."

"Mom, please let me spend time with my dad."

"Justin, I don't know. You have homework and you need to be rested before school starts."

"Please Mom."

"Mary Lou, I'll bring him back in a few hours. We just want to have a little father-son time together."

"Justin, can I trust you to call me? I want you back on time."

"Okay, Mom, I'll call."

"Do you know the number?"

Justin affirmed with an eye-rolling, "Yesssss, I know the number."

"You're old enough to call me if you're going to be late."

"I know, I know."

The other visitors looked on. I thought I saw thinly disguised smirks on their faces. Or maybe it was amusement.

"John I'm trusting you to do the right thing. Bring him back on time."

"I promise I will."

Justin gleefully rushed to his bedroom and emerged ready to go. As they were leaving I walked to the door with them asking, "John, what time will you have Justin back?"

"In just a few hours."

"Justin call me."

"Okay, Mom."

"John where are you staying?"

"The Best Western off Apopka-Vineland Road."

"John, I'm letting him go with you, but stick to your word and bring him home this evening before it gets late."

It was late, Friday night. John didn't bring Justin home. Justin didn't call. I tried to calm down enough to look up all Best Western numbers. I called them all, realizing I could only ask for John Lyonns because I didn't know the last names of the other two guys. It was John's habit to use his name but maybe he did something different this time. Maybe he used a fictitious name? I had allowed my son to go off with John and two men I did not know. I HAD NO IDEA WHERE THEY WERE! Mike was in the living room watching a football game while I frantically made calls. I suffocated my sobs into a pillow. Finally, I washed my face and tried to look normal. I walked into the living room, but before I could speak, tears betrayed me by welling into my eyes as I told Mike, "It's late. Justin's not home and I can't find him."

He walked over and embraced me. He tried to console me as the water welled up in my eyes and flowed freely and openly.

We talked about what we could do. After a while of thinking through the untenable mess, I told him, "Don't worry, go to bed and rest. I'll call every hotel until I find them."

I doubt he slept, but he did go to the bedroom. I stayed up late calling other hotels. In a tourist town like Orlando, it could take days to telephone all the hotels. I woke up in the morning with my face lying in the phone book.

I decided on an alternate approach and repeatedly telephoned John's parents hoping they would know how to contact him. The answering machine picked up each time. John was impossible to reach. Sunday, the phone finally rang. Justin called from the guard gate asking me to let them in. It turns out they had not stayed at a Best Western. John had taken Justin to a Disney hotel property. They had a grand time at Disney World. That was John—always interested in fun and good times. That was it for me! Being fair for my child's sake had its limits. I had reached the end of my concern for fairness, reasonableness AND access. I realized a father has to be worthy of honor and respect. Not all men who produce off-spring earn the title of father. John didn't come to the door but I saw him in the car. When he dropped Justin off, it was the last time I saw him, but his impact on Justin remained with us.

CHAPTER EIGHT

Tom, Tom, The Piper's Son

> Tom, Tom, the piper's son
> Stole a pig, and away he run,
> The pig was eat,
> And Tom was beat,
> And Tom ran crying down the street.
>
> —Mother Goose

In some respects, things seemed to take a normal course. Justin developed a serious crush on Sharon, one of his classmates. He opined, "She's not like the other girls. She's nice and studious."

Sharon walked by one evening when I was at the school to pick Justin up. He called her over and introduced us. She seemed a little shy and appeared to like him but I wasn't sure it was in the way he liked her. I agreed, "She's nice ...

and cute."

He had a crush the way only a fifteen-year-old can have on a first love. It was clear she had captured his heart.

In other ways, I wasn't so sure we were on the right track. I'd think I put money on a dresser or table in the bedroom but then it wasn't there. Maybe I was misremembering. Maybe the money was misplaced. On the first bank teller occurrence, we went to the bank then ran errands. By the time we got home, $100 dollars was missing. We called the bank teller to question whether she miscounted. She promised to call back when her drawer was closed. She did. She verified she had not miscounted.

I asked Justin, "Are you taking money from me?"

"I would never take money from you."

"Mike and I are married now and any money we have is combined, so we can achieve our goals. If you take money from Mike, you are stealing from me."

Huffily, "I wouldn't take money from you!

Our routine was to do a thorough cleaning on Saturdays. I went into Justin's room to check his work when I discovered a receipt for a dozen roses and limousine service stuffed in a football shaped cup on his dresser. After my shock, my first thought was how did he get money to do these things?! He clearly was trying to secure Sharon's affection. All those times of thinking Mike or I had misplaced money came together. The receipt was tangible evidence I could confront him with. He was put on punishment. No telephone calls, no after school activities, no weekend sports, no TV for two weeks.

It seemed he was on punishment for disobedient acts more than he was off. I began to look for small windows of good behavior to give him a little freedom. So, one Sunday, I let him go to the community clubhouse to play pool and socialize. He responded by staying out until the wee hours of the morning. He was put on punishment again.

Late November, I let Justin attend a football game after school, so he could socialize and enjoy some of the school year. We went to pick him up but he was not there. We searched around for several minutes. The crowd had nearly cleared out. I asked the police officer on duty, "Have you seen a young man with short wavy hair, about 6'2, he was wearing an olive green shirt and blue jeans?"

"I've seen your son around the school grounds some days after school, but I didn't see him tonight."

I desperately asked people as they left. No luck. While I attempted a calm disposition, I imagine anyone observing could see my anxiety; some showed pity on their faces. We walked around the stadium and the school until everyone was gone. No Justin. My stomach and mind churned in opposite directions and my level of existence dropped to a lower level. Mike offered, "Maybe he got a ride home."

We went home; he was not there. I called the police department to file a missing person's report. They refused to take the report because Justin had not been missing twenty-four hours. I insisted and after repeated calls and a few transfers, a community service officer came to our home and filed the report.

I called Sharon to see if she knew anything. She gave me the name of a guy Justin was hanging out with and the street where he lived; she didn't know the address.

Mike and I left home early Saturday morning in search of Justin. We lost our way and asked a police officer, "Do you know where Circlegrove St. is located? We're looking for our son and we think he is with Donny Johnson."

The officer raised his eyebrows. "If he is with Donny Johnson, that is not a good sign."

Mike asked, "You know him?"

"Oh yeah, we know him well. He is often in trouble. He lives with his mother who is blind."

He gave us directions and wished us luck. Mike and I found the address but Justin wasn't anywhere in sight. I got out of the car and knocked on the door. Mike was right behind me on the steps. The boy, maybe it was Donny, said he had not seen Justin. But something about his posture and how quickly he said, "I haven't seen him," made Mike and I wonder if he was telling the truth.

We returned to the school to look around. Still—no answers. Sunday evening, the Seminole County police department called and said he was in their lobby. I didn't know the location of the station so Mike went with me. The station reception area was all glass. We could see Justin slouched in a chair as we drove up.

We identified ourselves to the officer then Mike said, "We'll take this piece of trash off your hands now."

The air was sucked out of the room. It felt as if Mike had plunged a large knife into my heart. I was surprised and hurt to the core to hear those words coming from the man I had married. Worst of all, Justin heard him. A passing officer had stopped in his tracks. All who heard the comment stopped for a beat. The passing officer held his hand up to the desk officer that he would take over. The concerned officer took Mike and me to a room. He started, "I have a wonderful relationship with my son. Do you know how we established it?"

Mike shook his head.

"I spend time with him doing things that we like to do."

He offered suggestions then encouraged, "Just try a few things and see how it goes."

Message to the Future

CHAPTER NINE

Three Children Sliding On The Ice

Three children sliding on the ice
Upon a summer's day,
As it fell out, they all fell in.
The rest they ran away.

Now had these children been at home,
Or sliding on dry ground,
Ten thousand pounds to one penny
They had not all be drowned.

You parents all that children have,
And you have got none,
If you would have them safe abroad,
Pray keep them safe at home.

—Mother Goose

It was a quiet ride home. My inquiries were responded to with generalities. At twelve, my son had been a sweet, helpful child. I could not believe that this was the same boy. However, I thought I saw a glimmer of hope with the officer's comments. They made sense. In the privacy of our bedroom, I pleaded with Mike to take Justin out to fish or play basketball or something. Mike had never been married, had no children and had been blessed to live in a stable, two parent family in a somewhat sheltered environment. He could only draw from his childhood experience. All he knew is what his father would have done. He told me, "I don't believe in rewarding someone for bad behavior. Justin knows right from wrong. When he is good for a period of time, I will take him someplace. That's how my father raised me."

I explained, "You were with your father all your life. This is different."

Definitively he responded, "Right is right and wrong is wrong."

I began to realize the color-coordinated pieces I tried to carefully fit together in deciding to remarry were changing shades before my eyes. I had just moved us to a new state. Should I divorce him so quickly? Mike's lack of experience and insight were limiting him and causing problems. I thought if John and the Lyonnses would just not encourage Justin's dissatisfaction, he would develop a decent relationship with Mike and he could grow into a responsible person.

Eventually, Mike and his friend, Gary, took Justin to play basketball. Justin had expressed an interest in playing on the team at school. I was delighted to hear of his interest because he had found a place of comfort in the past through team sports.

I asked them both about the outing. My conversation with each of them resulted in different perspectives. Mike believed, "He is an okay player, but he seems lazy and he's a know-it-all."

Justin was more positive, "It was alright. I might start lifting weights with Gary."

When I spoke to Gary, an Orange County, Florida, Sheriff, he offered to have him spend a night in jail under his supervision to scare him into getting on track. I wouldn't do that. There were too many possibilities of something going wrong. I was concerned about the psychological effects given his dad's incarcerations. I was worried beyond belief. I sat on the couch trying to think my way to a successful outcome. I flipped through the phone book looking for counselors. On the back of the Orlando phone book was an advertisement for a hospital for troubled teens. I called and asked what services they offered. The lady described the program. No matter how reasonable she made it sound, I could only envision my child being drugged to be kept under control or in some way mistreated. It was an option my heart would not allow me to take.

I didn't nag Mike to do anything with Justin again. I wanted him to try to bond with him on his own accord. I didn't want to create more resentment in him or subject my child to cold treatment.

Justin had to stay at school a couple hours, before we could pick him up. He was to use that time to study. I was pleased when he decided to spend his time after school trying out for the basketball team. I usually went into the gym to let Justin know we were outside waiting. One day, when I was bone tired, Mike went in alone to pick up Justin. He took that opportunity to ask the coach about Justin's progress. Justin told me he saw Mike talking to the coach, so I privately asked Mike what he said. Reportedly, the coach told him, "I'm wavering on whether or not to cut Justin from the team."

He asked, "What are the rules for playing with low grades?"

That conversation made the difference. Justin was cut from the team and I lost the last chance I could see of getting him involved in our new life.

When Mike disclosed his actions, I was livid, "Why in the world would you do that?"

"My parents didn't let me play basketball or any sport until my grades were up."

"That is asinine! Justin is not in the situation you grew up in. He hasn't been in a two-parent home all his life! It's good to have standards but this is different, he is trying to find a comfortable place!! You absolutely did the wrong thing. It would have been better for you to keep your mouth shut! Keep your opinions to yourself. Why didn't you talk to me about it before you did that?"

Matter-of-factly but defensively he replied, "I just thought it was the right thing to do. Grades are important."

"Really? Really!"

He just continued to sit on the side of the bed shining his shoes.

Even if he was right, Justin needed the game in a way he couldn't understand. He needed to belong and have success or failure be exclusively his. I couldn't undo it but I was certain the grades would have come had he just been able to engage.

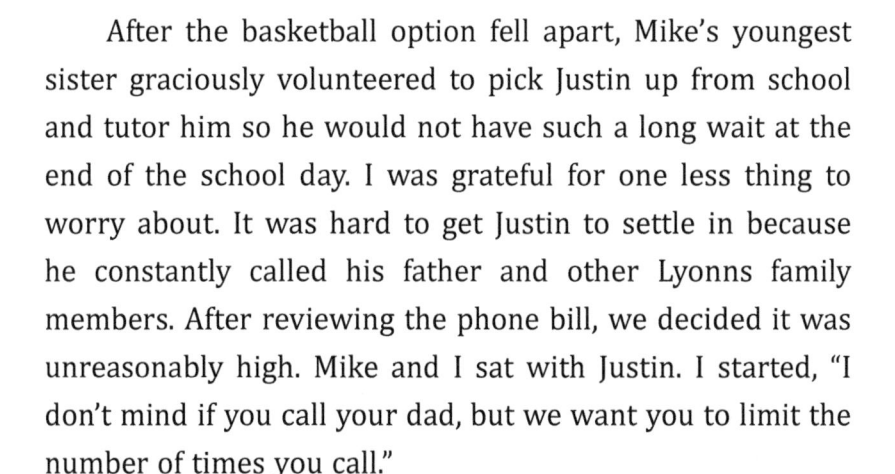

After the basketball option fell apart, Mike's youngest sister graciously volunteered to pick Justin up from school and tutor him so he would not have such a long wait at the end of the school day. I was grateful for one less thing to worry about. It was hard to get Justin to settle in because he constantly called his father and other Lyonns family members. After reviewing the phone bill, we decided it was unreasonably high. Mike and I sat with Justin. I started, "I don't mind if you call your dad, but we want you to limit the number of times you call."

"I just want to talk to him, since I can't be with him."

"That's okay, just call once a week, that's all."

He continued to secretly call his dad and the Lyonnses. We unplugged all the phones before we went to bed and took them into our bedroom. Justin continued to call the

Lyonnses collect from school. It appeared they were filling his head with all sorts of reasons why he shouldn't be happy in Florida. I couldn't stop him from calling them from school.

I felt Justin and I needed to spend time alone to continue connecting in new and old ways in our new home. I dedicated more time alone with him. Mike's mom, Mrs. Lamm, invited us for Thanksgiving dinner with the family. I declined the invitation for Justin and I but encouraged Mike to go alone. He said he wanted his family with him. Eventually, he reluctantly went alone. Justin and I went to Straub's, one of our favorite restaurants. The Lyonns family continued to accept his collect calls and listen to his criticisms. They allied with him against the adjustments I was trying to get him to make. I called my family and friends looking for support, trying to determine the best path to help him. My closest brother, Loren, offered, "Send him to me."

"Thank you but I don't want to pass my problems off on you."

"It would be no trouble, sis."

My brother was kind, honest and among the most principled people I knew, but I didn't want to burden anyone else. One of my friends suggested, "Call Mrs. Lyonns and tell them to butt out."

I finally took her advice and called the matriarch, "Ms. Lyonns, I know Justin is complaining about how awful things are for him. But please be assured he is not being mistreated and I am working with him. I don't want him to feel he can get sympathy elsewhere when I'm trying to guide him to a good place in life."

She doubtfully said, "I understand." I was sure all in that matriarchal family would hear of the telephone conversation because that is how they operated. Yet, they continued to accept collect calls, listened and supported Justin. He seemed to think of them as his saviors.

Mike did try. On the days we drove him to and from school, he initiated or engaged in discussions about echelons of society, how people selected their place in life by the choices they made. Principles of living in the world and many other topics we thought up. One day, I said, "Justin you are my message to the future. All the things I am telling you and teaching you will live on into the future after my death. All my hopes, dreams and good intentions are invested in you."

"I understand."

I now know—he did not understand.

Message to the Future

CHAPTER TEN

Butterfly, Butterfly

> Butterfly, butterfly,
> Whence do you come?
> "I know not, I ask not, nor ever had a home."
> Butterfly, butterfly,
> Where do you go?
> "Where the sun shines, and where the buds grow."
>
> —Mother Goose

The Lyonns' support reached a crescendo in December 1990. Lisa Lyonns, Justin's tiny-waisted, large bottomed, bouncy bartender aunt called telling Justin, "There will be a ticket for you at the Delta airline counter. The password is "Coming Home."

Excitedly he told me, "Mom I want to go."

Surprised and hurt I protested, "But you've always spent Christmas with me."

"I'll get to see my dad. I want to go."

Depressed, I sat in his room and played Sade's "Maureen" and Stephanie Mills' "Coming Home" while he packed his clothes. Before heading to the airport, I took him to "Blackies," a Mexican restaurant he liked. Hugged him and with a broken heart sent him to Toledo.

I called frequently, "Justin you need to get back to restart school on time; come home right away. We can have a good life in Florida if we all just try."

"My family wants me to stay here."

He may have enjoyed Christmas day in Toledo, but each day I spoke with him, it was clear he was not getting what he expected. During our telephone conversations, I discovered he did not see his dad as much as he had hoped. I convinced him to return home to Florida. The second semester of school had started. It didn't appear to me that the Lyonnses were genuinely interested in his well-being, yet for some reason, they did not want to see us move on.

He was definitely different when he came back. His actions were erratic. He was making behavioral choices I could never imagine my sweet child would make. It started with benign aberrations that grew into increasingly more malevolent actions.

He always had plausible explanations for what happened. He received detentions for talking during class. I thought it was a result of him being a new student at the school and children testing and or teasing him. He left the school grounds for lunch one day. I thought it was an accidental infraction, because high school students were allowed off campus during lunch in Toledo. Then, he began to steal at school. Someone accused him of taking five dollars from a locker. He swore he hadn't done it. He told us he was near the locker and they assumed he took the money. I could not say whether he was telling the truth or not, which scared me. The string of occurrences had me beginning to doubt him. I wanted him to adjust into the safe, easy flow of the life I envisioned.

At some point it became undeniable that he was lying to cover up his actions. At first, I thought I just misplaced the camera. I thought I had not put the twenty dollars on our dresser or had already used the small, cash stash I kept in a drawer. One Friday, on our way home from work and school, I saw Mike place a hundred dollar bill and some receipts on the floorboard of the car. I was sitting in the front seat the entire time while Mike made a few stops. Just before heading home Mike looked around, searching for the money asking, "Did anyone see the hundred dollar bill I left on the floor mat?"

"No, but why do you leave money on the floor of the car? It is not safe. It could be knocked out when you get out, or someone might look in and see it. It just invites problems."

Mike didn't respond to my reminder to change a bad habit.

He asked, "Justin did you see the money?"

I spoke into the silence, "Justin did you see or move the

money that was under the floor mat?"

"No."

"Are you sure?"

"Yes."

Mike thought maybe some error had been made at the credit union. He drove back to discuss the error with the teller. She retraced the transaction with him and assured him she gave him the money. Justin and I stayed in the car while Mike retraced his steps. He finally concluded there was nothing more to do but go home. Justin remained silent throughout the search.

Message to the Future

CHAPTER ELEVEN

London Bridge

London Bridge is falling down, falling down,
My fair lady
How shall we build it up again? Build it up again,
My fair lady
Build it up with silver and gold, silver and gold,
Silver and gold will be stole away, My fair lady
Build it up with iron and steel, iron and steel,
Iron and steel will bend and bow, My fair lady
Build it up with wood and clay, wood and clay,
Wood and clay will wash away, My fair lady.
Build it up with stone so strong, stone so strong,
Huzza! Twill last for ages long, My fair lady

—Mother Goose

February 1991, Justin came home from school and handed me a flier. "They're having a rally at one the local high schools. I really want to go to the event."

I read the flier. It had text about life, death and had religious connotations. He also had a book by Jerry Johnson titled *Why Suicide?* I read through parts of it and became very concerned.

"Where did you get this book?"

"It was on a table at school and I took it."

I thought it odd that he would be compelled to take such a book, so I knew I had to take him to the meeting. I asked Mike for directions and just Justin and I went to the meeting. A church sponsored the rally, so I thought the goal was to get new members. I looked around the stadium and saw the young people were really touched by what Mr. Johnson was saying. I looked over at Justin and tears were running down his face. I put my arms around him asking, "What's wrong?"

Crying, he said, "I don't know. I just feel bad."

"About what?"

He paused for a long time then said, "About myself"

"What caused it?"

Another long pause and he eventually said, "I don't know."

He didn't want to talk and I didn't want to press him, so I said, "We have to pray. Talk to the Lord and you'll feel better."

As soon as I said those words, the meeting was also ending in prayer. We went to the podium so he could speak to Jerry Johnson. The crowd was so thick, it was impossible to get to him. We walked to another area and picked up a slice of pizza and a soda. A young helper came around and started talking to us. She offered some literature and Justin took it! He was usually not interested in church. It often was a major push to get him to sit and read the Bible with me. He exchanged telephone numbers with the young lady and gave her our address. She promised to write and call him. Justin had a pained look on his face. I couldn't think of why he was feeling so dejected. My heart hurt.

On the ride home, I gingerly tried to talk more about the rally, school and finding a church we liked. Justin was quiet and sullen. I wanted to do anything to make him feel better and find out why he felt so bad.

When I got home, I picked up *Why Suicide?* and read the section on indicators of suicidal thoughts. I committed them to memory and committed myself to looking out for any signs. For a few weeks, Justin communicated and met with the people from the church, then suddenly became disinterested. I knew a move and a stepfather was all a lot to adjust to, but I figured I was always there right beside him. I decided Justin needed to think more highly of his angular face with its high bridge nose and intelligent kind eyes. In my mind, his wavy hair and lean body all put him squarely on the gorgeous scales. So, I focused on praising him for the good parts of his character and his positive actions. I would try not to criticize him at all. It was a reasonable plan but a challenge to implement when he kept getting into trouble. My son was not only physically handsome but also had a good mind. It was hard to believe he didn't think highly of himself.

Message to the Future

CHAPTER TWELVE

To Babylon

"How many miles is it to Babylon?"
Threescore miles and ten.
"Can I get there by candlelight?"
Yes, and back again.
If your heels are nimble and light
You may get there by candlelight.

—Mother Goose

During one of our Saturday afternoon cleanings in February, I heard Mike in Justin's bathroom say, "Be sure to clean this area of the shower."

Then I heard the bathroom door slam shut. I struggled to open the door but could not. I shouted, "Open the door! What are you doing in there? Justin...? Mike..."

No reply. I left the condo to get the guard to help me open the door. I had always handled things on my own so I felt I should have been able to handle this, halfway there, I turned around. The bathroom door was open. I went directly to Justin's room. "What happened?"

Justin showed me a reddening area on his shoulder. I again asked, "What happened?"

"I was reaching for the sponge to clean the area Mike showed me. Then Mike pushed me against the wall."

"Did he hit you?"

"No."

"What did he do?"

"He pushed me against the wall and held me there."

I thought Mike was 6'4" and a trim 210 pounds and Justin was 6'2" but he was a youthful, thin guy. Justin had never been violent. He was uncharacteristically disobedient but never violent. I had not known Mike to be violent either; yet I didn't know him as well as I knew my son. Mike's lack of understanding was becoming a real problem. I was furious.

My ire turned to Mike. "Why did you pin Justin to the wall?"

His response was defensive, "I thought he was going to hit me."

"Really? Has he ever been violent? Have you ever seen that in him?"

"No, but I've not seen this kind of disrespectful behavior either. He just seems like a different person."

Almost pleading I said, "I agree; but he is not violent."

He said matter-of-factly, "Well he knows right from wrong."

"He does but he's got a big adjustment here."

Again matter-of-factly, "Well, all I know to do is what my father would do."

It was my turn to be huffy and matter-of-fact as I replied, "That's different. You've lived all your life with your father. It's not the same! Don't ever touch him again!"

A couple days later Justin advised, "I told one of my teachers about what happened in the bathroom and she reported it as abuse. I didn't ask her to, but she said she had to. She said I don't have to put up with that treatment."

"I agree."

Mike was already stopping by his mother's house in the evenings after work. But I decided Justin and I needed alone time out of our home. We started going to the neighborhood library every evening. I noticed he checked out poetry, writing and teenager's rights books. In a few days, I received a call from Ms. Rae from the Florida Health and Rehabilitative Services Department (HRS). I believe in children's rights and was glad he had an advocate who cared enough to investigate. Ms. Rae made an appointment to visit our home so she could get a sense of our family dynamics.

Ms. Rae was a well-worn investigator. Not old, but she definitely looked experienced. She arrived on a Friday evening and we all sat at the oval- shaped, black-lacquered dining room table. All was well during the meeting until Ms. Rae threatened me saying, "The Florida HRS will put you in jail if Mike or you ever hit Justin again."

I didn't defend myself because I had righteously spanked him before, but I naively asked, "Even if I spank him as punishment for doing something wrong?"

"Yes."

After her response, I sat staring across the room thinking. Mike had never gotten involved in disciplining Justin; he just watched. My son was taller than me and outweighed me. He was old enough that my attempts to whip his behind resulted in hurt feeling more than physical pain and seemingly re-established I was the parent and the one in control. However, any perceived balance of power tilted with Ms. Rae's threat to me, and clearly neutered my authority. I thought, *I am being emasculated in front of my son. The Florida HRS is effectively telling Justin I cannot raise him as I see fit.* I further translated it into: *My son can run over me, disregard my guidance and do whatever he wants.* Heat rose in my body as my thoughts continued: *In the eyesight of the Florida HRS I can only feed, clothe and talk and if talking doesn't work, too bad; deal with his behavior.* Those mental calculations devolved to, *I have no power, I need to move from this state.* I could feel my body getting hot. My attempts to maintain my composure failed as tears rolled down my face. My voice was loud and forceful as I yelled, "Then you take him! Take him tonight! Right now! Do not leave without him because you will have to jail me in the future, if you don't take him now! I will NOT say that I will never hit him and if that is what you want; you-all raise him. I punish when I can and when all else fails, I reserve the right to spank. I don't slap him or knock him around, but I beat his behind when necessary."

I loved my child and had probably only spanked him six or seven times in his entire life. But I was not willing to say I would never do it, especially not in front of him! I thought about how over the years some observers didn't think I disciplined him enough. *I didn't think I needed to because love usually provided the best results. However, I knew from my own experience as a child there were times nothing else worked. I was a good child but I would continue to stretch the limits of my curfew as long as I knew I could promise to do better and not suffer consequences. But even the punishments of going to my room without television, radio and no friends for extended periods of times didn't faze me. Those things didn't bother me, I could always read or look out the window. We had a large family and we always ate together that was plenty socializing for me. Even if we had the room to have me eat alone, that would have been fine with me. There really was no other effective punishment I could have been given to change my behavior. The number of times I needed a physical wake-up call were few and far between, but there were times, I know, I certainly needed them. And, in our home, respect for our parent was foundational, so there was no verbal challenging. Now I was being told I could never use corporal punishment on my own child. I could no longer parent according to what I determined was the best route.*

Everyone around the table was staring at me. Justin looked nervous and uncomfortable. Ms. Rae twisted in her seat and looked as if she couldn't think of a thing to say. She offered no alternative approaches. Mike's face reflected pure surprise. His eyes were wide, head slightly cocked, neck pulled back and he looked at me as if I had lost my mind. I didn't care. I was truly angry. I knew I had been the best mother that I could be. I also felt really confident Justin understood his life with me had been pretty damn good and he wouldn't want to give it up to be with strangers.

Through more tears I asked, "Are you going to stop the police officer from beating him with a nightstick or shooting him later in life? Are you going to make sure you're around to question the officer about abuse? Do you think police officers are going to ask the HRS for permission before beating him unmercifully?"

Ms. Rae just looked at me; astonished. Then, she dared to repeat, "You are not to hit him."

There didn't seem to be any reasoning with Florida law. I hoarsely yelled, "You go, and take him with you. If you think you can love him, care for him and raise him better than I can, then do it! Take him!"

Justin's face was strained. To calm the fury I felt, I got up from my seat and went to the bedroom to put a cold, wet towel on my face. I heard Justin go into his bedroom and close the door. From our bedroom, I could hear Mike calmly and quietly speaking to Ms. Rae. I couldn't hear what they were saying, but I felt humiliated that Mike had to handle the situation. He was trying to tell Ms. Rae about *my* son and me. He could not possibly know what to say. Justin was mine. He was my responsibility. I marched out of our bedroom and into Justin's room telling him he needed to accompany me back to the table so we could hear what was being said. He reluctantly left his room with me.

Mike was promising, "I will never touch Justin again."

Ms. Rae stood up and pointedly replied, "I recommend counseling for Justin. In fact, the entire family should be counseled together."

I remained seated at the table as she prepared to depart. She turned to me and handed me a card. Ms. Rae advised, "Call the number on the card to schedule appointments with a counselor."

Then she started with another threat, "If you don't call within..."

My eyes flashed and Mike stepped forward assuring Mrs. Rae "Don't worry we will call before the end of the week."

Our home felt tight and confined with tension. I encouraged Mike to participate in counseling with us but he worked late and was always too busy. A couple weeks later, I decided Justin and I would get started, Mike could join in later. I called the number and scheduled a counselor visit to our home.

Welcoming, but also a little apprehensively, I opened the door and scanned the face and body of the young, chubby, blond counselor standing confidently before me. A white and navy pinstriped, button down shirt framed her lightly tanned face. The scratch on the right toe of her comfortable-looking brown shoes looked fresh. She looked as if she just graduated from college. I asked if she had identification or paperwork associated with us. She breezily offered her state ID card. I led her to the chair with the view of the entire condo. She used the overstuffed arms of the chair to ease her ample bottom into the cushiony seat. Skin toned stockings peeked from under the navy no press pants.

I took the seat at the end of the couch closest to her and Justin sat next to me. She took in the matching grey, mauve and black furniture.

"You have a very nice place."

Her eyes scanned the two of us on the sofa then she shared, "I work with another family situation similar to yours. The father decided to remarry but he wanted his son to live with him. The father bought a beautiful home. However, the son didn't like his new step-mother, so he totally trashed their home."

Justin and I looked at each other uncomfortably. The counselor shook her head as she continued, "The son kicked big, gaping holes in the walls. He took a knife and cut open the backs and seats of all the furniture then threw the insides all over the house. He took a hammer and bashed in the TV, stereo and radios. The amount of destruction in that house was amazing! I could tell he was really angry!"

I sat stunned as she continued to describe the trashing of one of her client's home. It was unbelievable that she would share such a story with us upon introduction. I could feel Justin tensing up beside me. The counselor went on to explain, "The father and son are in a special program to work out family dynamics. I'd like you and your son to enroll in the program. Usually, a group of parents and children sit in a circle with a counselor and discuss family issues. I think it would be helpful for you guys to share your problems. "

That was it. She stopped talking and looked at us smiling. I turned to Justin and could see the shock that I felt was displayed on his face. I stood and calmly thanked her for coming. "We'll consider what you've told us."

I opened the door to let her out; February's fresh air entered the room as the counselor left.

I asked, "You feel like going to the Crab Shack?"

Contemplatively, he agreed.

We settled in our booth and talked about the counselor and her story. Justin opined, "That boy totally disrespected his father."

I exhaled a soft stream of relief between my lips. I was relieved that my son still had common sense and did not condone such behavior. I knew he hadn't settled into a comfort zone yet but he did not hate me or Mike. I couldn't see how such a counseling experience would help us. I never pursued it further, a month later we moved to a house we had been building in a different Florida county. I never heard from the Florida HRS again.

CHAPTER THIRTEEN

A Hopeless Case

> "What is the use" quoth the Whitewash Brush
> "I'll comb my hair no more;
> For try as I will to make it lie,
> It still stays pompadour"
>
> —Mother Goose

I had discovered I was pregnant in late January. I did not want to tell Justin. It would just be one more thing to deal with. But I knew I would have to tell him sometime before I started showing.

We were building a new home and stopped by often to see the progress. During one of these visits, Justin selected his bedroom. Most weekends and some weekday nights, all three of us went shopping for furniture for our home. Justin was bored but I didn't want to leave him out and needed to know where he was and what he was doing. He had wanted a pool so I insisted one be added. Mike countered, "It will add a lot of extra expense to the mortgage. If we add it on later outside of the mortgage it will cost us less..." He went on and on about it but I stood firm and said, "I'm working to pay for this house too and I want a pool." In March, we moved into the new house. Justin was excited to move in and seemed happy when I encouragingly reminded him, "We built this pool just for you."

One evening I went into his room and told him I was going to have a baby. He raised his eyebrows but didn't say much.

It was clear Justin was still stealing. We didn't know what to do. I asked Mike, "Just stop bringing cash home."

"That's ridiculous. I should be comfortable at home if nowhere else."

I couldn't argue with that. While Mike was making mistakes, he was genuinely a personable, responsible, caring person. He spent lots of time looking for suitable furnishings for our home. He was a great provider and we almost always ate meals together. I believed the stable existence I wanted for Justin could be experienced with Mike. I thought he could guide Justin to be the man I wanted him to become.

Justin could now ride the bus and walk home from school but we didn't give him a key so he had to do his homework in the garage or on the patio until we got home. Theoretically, he would have his homework done and be free in the evening. After a few weeks, he befriended a schoolmate in the neighborhood. He visited with him after school. The child's parents liked him too, so sometimes I had to go to their home to bring Justin home. One day, I mentioned, "Larry seems disrespectful, I don't care for him."

Justin stifled an emotion as he almost whined, "He is the only one who will have me over. He has a step-parent also, so he gets me."

He was not able to get into the house after school and I spoke against the one guy who helped him. I felt guilty for saying anything. It didn't feel right to have him not be in the house even for a short time.

As had always been the case, wherever we lived, the neighbors liked Justin. He was just an amicable person with a friendly grin and courteous conversation. He took the initiative to get a job cutting our neighbor's lawn. He proudly disclosed,

"I made an offer then negotiated the job with her."

I smiled, "Good job! I knew you were an entrepreneur at heart."

Several seldom used items, like extra phones, cameras and other objects continued to disappear from our home. I decided my punishments were not effective or enough, so I took a different tactic. When he did something wrong, I had him write an essay about it. He wrote essays on lying, stealing, honesty, dishonesty, obedience, or whatever the situation required. He didn't like writing the papers but he covered the subjects very well in the two or three required paragraphs. It was very clear that he knew what he was doing, but why he chose to continue the behavior wasn't clear. I walked into his room one weekend evening and saw the word "bitch" etched into the top casing of his TV. I stood stunned staring at it for a long time. I told Mike, "I can't believe Justin would etch anything into furniture especially not a curse word."

Mike agreed, "His behavior has not been like anything I've seen from him."

There had been two or three suspensions from school. I usually asked Mrs. Lamm to let him stay with her. But I decided not to intrude further, during his last three-day suspension. I told Justin to stay home while we were at work and not have any company. He and his buddy Larry had other ideas; they went to a beach. He stole a set of hotel keys and money from the beach at a hotel. He also made long distance calls from the hotel. The manager traced the telephone calls and other activity and called us. We paid the bill and once we found the keys, we returned them.

Something had to be done to wake Justin up to where this dark spiral of his behavior was leading. I had talked to him about so many things in so many ways that I wasn't sure what to do next. I thought maybe a logical, visible depiction would help. I worked on a timeline from 1986 to 1991 listing occurrences of inappropriate or bad behavior. I framed the chart by school year and titled it *Behavior Trend*. In putting it together, it dawned on me, the time frame coincided with him becoming a teenager, Angela's death and my engagement and marriage to Mike. At the far end of the chart was a column for consequences.

May 1991, I was six months pregnant when I sat down with him. I started, "Your behaviors are spiraling out of control. I want to know why you've been doing these things. I also want to know how I can help you change and improve."

I went through three points on the chart; then just stopped. It was too depressing. "This is ridiculous. Justin, I know you know better and I know you can do better. I want you to have the things you want in life, but you have to work for them. Even drug dealers have to work, and then when they acquire things, they can never be comfortable. Drug dealers always have to look over their shoulders for the police, a crazy druggie or someone trying to take over their business."

I paused. He looked towards me and the charts but didn't comment.

"Justin, I know you want to travel and do the kind of things we've done together and that means you need an education so that you can afford to do them legally."

He finally spoke up, "I'll start my own business. I'll work with dad in a barber shop."

"That could work; but I'd like you to dream bigger. Look at the people around you, people you know. Who is leading the kind of life you would like to live? Who is doing the kinds of things you would like to do? All of them have college degrees."

We went through names of people we knew, family members and situations. He looked at me directly and seemed to non-verbally agree.

After a few minutes, he turned slightly and made a shrug of his shoulder. It seemed to be a dismissal of what I was saying.

We sat quietly for a while. He finally said, "My main goal in my negative behavior is to be allowed to go live with my dad."

"I don't want you to go. It's not a stable environment for consistency in school. There are drugs around and I don't think you will do your homework. I don't think it's a good idea."

"Then I'll just keep doing things until you let me go."

"I'm not going to do it. If your dad wanted you to come live with him, he would take a drug test, allow case worker visits, periodic drug testing, and keep a real job. He hasn't done any of that so you can't go."

My son gave me a look I had never seen before; he looked at me as if he hated me!

"I hope the baby dies."

I was surprised. Not by his comment; I knew he loved children. He had always helped others, stood up for them when they were attacked for being small, different or because they just didn't fit in. He had always been a right-minded person. But the look of anger—almost hatred—was something I had never seen and never thought I would see from my sweet son.

Justin complained to his dad about Mike when we caught him stealing another $100.

He later reported, "My dad said he will kill Mike."

It was obvious; John was still spewing negativity and actively supporting bad behavior.

I knew I had to do something. I went to his room and asked, "How would you feel about the two of us living at the condo? We could live there for a while and maybe things will get better."

"No, Mom, I want you to be happy."

I thought my pregnancy might have had some bearing on his response. So I started working out the logistics of how it could be done.

Justin listened and compassionately just said, "No, I want to go. I don't want to make things difficult for you."

CHAPTER FOURTEEN

Star Light, Star Bright

> Star light, star bright, first star I see tonight,
> Wish I may, wish I might, have this wish I wish tonight.
>
> ***
>
> Star light, star bright, first star I see tonight.
> Won't you make my dreams come true?
>
> Star light, star bright, first star I see tonight.
> Can't you hear my plea to you?
> Won't you make my dreams come true?
>
> —Mother Goose

I grudgingly admitted there was less tension in the house; we no longer had to make every move or plan considering what Justin would do. Yet I missed him.

After Justin left, Mike's grandmother said she wouldn't choose a man over her child. She didn't know the half of what had transpired but the comment hurt. I'm sure it looked that way to her and others. Yet, I didn't see it that way at all. Mike was definitely a good man. Like everyone, he had his shortcomings and one of them happened to be lack of experience in anything other than a homogenous family. I felt if I could just get John to step back the Lyonns family would follow suit and we could work with Justin to have a more carefree life with a positive trajectory. I didn't respond when Mike's grandmother made the comment, but the remark hit its target—straight in my heart.

I called Justin, wrote encouraging letters filled with love and pride and sent self-esteem building cards, but Justin never wrote back. It took him three months to finally call me teasing, "That baby better not be born on my birthday."

"The baby could be your birthday present; a real live present." We laughed. When she finally was born, he asked for a picture and showed it off to his family and acquaintances in Toledo. He even drew a sketch of her from the picture. His art instructors always said he had an artistic eye. We established a pattern of calling every day or so. On his birthday he complained, "Granny didn't make me a cake."

"She made your favorite banana pudding earlier in the week."

"Yeah, but that's not the same. I didn't get a cake *on* my birthday."

"Well some people view birthdays differently from what you're accustomed to."

He had cards and money from my mother and me, yet I could hear he missed the customs we had established.

To not cause his grandparents any additional expense, I gave them my insurance card for any medical or dental care Justin might need. I also asked that they advise me of any book or school expenses. Each month, I sent a small maintenance amount to Mrs. Lyonns. It seemed his grandparents were being attentive. Mr. Lyonns took Justin to school every morning. He attended church on a regular basis with one of his cousins. In October, Justin reported, "Granny is complaining about me being on the phone and she says I'm running up her telephone bill."

I advised, "Complete your homework before talking on the phone. Don't create problems. Always call me collect; and don't call Sharon without permission. It's been a long time since they've had a teenager in their home."

Early November, I flew to Ohio on a business trip. I made arrangements for Mother to drive Justin to Ohio so we could spend the weekend together. Lisa Lyonns answered when I called to arrange the pick-up time. She informed, "Justin has been tardy to his classes and he has to go to school for Saturday detention. He can't come to Ohio to see you."

I was stunned, but simply said, "Okay." I knew I could not be so close and not see my son. I drove to Toledo, took him to the detention and when that was over, we were free. It was so much like old times and the loving relationship we always had that when I returned home, I told Mike, "I want Justin to come home."

He responded, "I thought this was a move to get him to

change his behavior? It hasn't been six months and you want him to come home."

I mumbled, "He's my son."

Thanksgiving evening, Justin called saying, "I'll never spend another holiday with the Lyonns family. All they did was talk negatively about me.

"All of them?"

"Any of them that didn't talk about me laughed at me."

It was something I had been afraid of. He was being treated as an outsider in that tight-knit clan. I tried to comfort him as best I could without saying anything negative. In the end, I offered, "When we can't be together, you can spend the holidays with Mother."

Not long after that Mike logically commented, "The phone bills are getting a little excessive. We're giving the phone company $400 every month in long distance calls."

In a fed up tone, I responded, "If the telephone bill is hundreds of dollars, that's okay, because some things cannot be compromised. I work to pay these bills too."

He didn't say anything more about telephone bills.

Looking for a brighter side, I thought Uncle Kerry and Aunt Isabelle might be supportive of Justin, they both were successful professionals and seemed to be reasonable people. I asked, "Have you been talking to Isabelle?"

"Yes, but there is not much to say."

"How about Kerry?"

"Some, but he isn't around much."

Then he opened up sounding as if he was in tears, "My dad is locked up for ten years."

"What did he do? Why so long?"

"Dad was with his cousin who was getting high. A police car came by and saw him. My dad wasn't doing anything. And anyway, I don't know how the police could see anyone in the car because the windows were tinted."

Surprised, I queried, "How do you know?"

"I was in the back seat of the car."

Alarms went off in my head, I exclaimed, "Your dad had you out under those circumstances? You could have been hurt!"

In his opinion, I overreacted and he changed the subject. "I have to help my little brother and sister. My dad's girlfriend, Lana, isn't giving my brother and sister the care that they need. I try to spend time with them and I really want to help them."

"That's admirable that you want to help, but I want you to concentrate on you. You can be a positive example for them. Justin, they'll be alright. Their mother will take care of them, just like I took care of you."

"She needs protection and guidance in caring for them. But I realize I can't do anything for myself now. I'm just trying to keep myself going right now."

"It'll be okay, someone in the Lyonns family will help them if they need it."

That seemed to calm him.

Christmas was approaching and I was concerned about Justin spending another holiday with the Lyonnses. Little Gabrielle was two months old and I wanted to spend this first special holiday with her. However, I reasoned she knew nothing of Christmas and Mike and his family would take good care of her. I was torn but on Christmas day I flew to Toledo to be with Justin. When I picked him up from the Lyonns' home, the glee on his face was inescapable. He was so happy and treated me like a precious gift. I stayed five days and just before I was to return, Justin opened up to me, "I don't like the fact that we are not together. We were doing alright before Mike came along. We had a home, a nice RX7 and each other. We had fun."

"I know. I wanted it to be even better and it could be. Mike could be a good role model if you gave him a chance."

Disagreeing he said, "Look at those old cars you are driving."

"Yes, but we have a nicer house now."

"Our old home was fine."

"We'll be upgrading at least one car before long. And remember, we have a pool now; we got that just for you."

"It doesn't make sense to have those old cars."

I thought I was giving him all that he wanted and needed to become a grounded, positive man. But it wasn't what he wanted at all.

Message to the Future

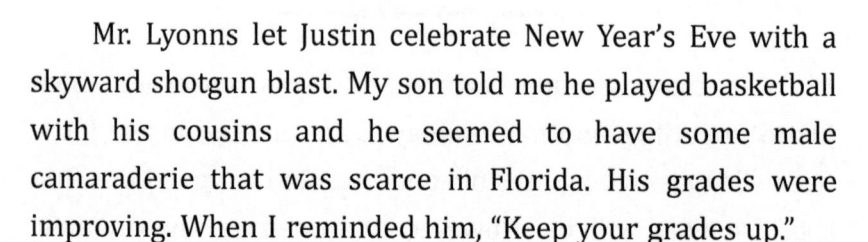

Mr. Lyonns let Justin celebrate New Year's Eve with a skyward shotgun blast. My son told me he played basketball with his cousins and he seemed to have some male camaraderie that was scarce in Florida. His grades were improving. When I reminded him, "Keep your grades up."

He proudly reported, "My report card is full of good grades."

I thought maybe I was wrong about him going to Toledo.

CHAPTER FIFTEEN

Curiouser and Curiouser

> "Curiouser and curiouser!" cried Alice (she was so much surprised, that for the moment she quite forgot how to speak good English)."
>
> — Lewis Carroll

Early in his stay in Toledo, Ms. Lyonns' attorney sent custody papers to me several times. Each time, I replied with modifications showing the custody was temporary. I was not giving away my parental rights. In fact, I never wanted him to be there. After four or five iterations with changes we never discussed, they finally stopped. The Lyonnses and I agreed temporary custody was needed in case he got ill or something. So, I was surprised the legal paperwork implied anything else. I now suspect it was to have me give up my rights so John could have full control at some point. But that is only a guess.

It was about nine months into Justin's life in Toledo, when a teacher left the art classroom and a student started pushing, criticizing and pestering Justin—that day in March 1992, he was finally fed up; he grabbed the student about the chest and arms and put a putty knife to his throat, reportedly saying, "Leave me alone!"

He was called to the counselor's office to be chastised.

<small>He explained he just wanted him to leave him alone.</small>

A rule was broken.

<small>He had not initiated the altercation. The other students will tell you.</small>

He had to be punished.

<small>That is unfair.</small>

And with that anger he hit a large, plate glass window.

It shattered everywhere.

He needed stitches in one of his fingers.

He was taken to the hospital for emergency care.

He could not return to school without a psychological evaluation.

He was referred to an out-patient support group for care.

When I heard about the incident, I asked, "What happened to the other boy?"

"Nothing. He's white, and his parents insisted he was innocent."

"Is your hand injured badly?"

"I had stitches; it'll be okay."

"Tell me about the counseling session."

"An adult is supposed to be with me at every session."

"I think I should be part of it, so I can give them information."

"I've got this."

"Have the counselor call me collect so I can talk to him."

No one called, so I called the hospital where the sessions were held and after many, many transfers I was told the counselors were not there and the head of the psychological group was on vacation. In typical fashion, I began to second-guess myself. Maybe Justin didn't want me involved; should I be involved? Ms. Lyonns hadn't said anything. I was reluctant to ask her because I felt she had accepted a burden on her son's behalf and I wanted to not add friction to it.

Justin said Ms. Lyonns went with him a couple of times and never went again. Mother went with him a couple of times also. She reported, "Justin is very, very knowledgeable about what should be done in difficult situations. He just doesn't use that same rationale when he encounters problems."

It seemed Justin was mostly on his own when he attended the sessions.

In May, he told me, "I'm sad to leave the group, but I know it's time to end with them."

Later, I found out more about what was said during those sessions.

Thankfully, Isabelle made arrangements for Justin to attend another high school. Ironically, it was the one I hoped he would attend from the beginning. I thought it was a better fit.

Mother observed, "Justin always seems upset after he visits his dad."

"He can't go without an adult. Who is taking him?"

"I believe Mr. Lyonns."

"Do you think his dad is putting demands on him or pressuring him in some way? Is he threatening to do things to him or someone? Or is it because he is sad to see his dad in prison?"

"I don't know. Justin won't talk to me about his visits with his dad. I tried to speak with him about it, but I was met with a wall of silence. No one can help because he won't talk. He is very protective of his dad."

There were many incidents that would not have been a factor in his life if he had been home with me. He complained, "Granny and Pawpaw won't sign for me to get my license."

He forged the signature and had a friend take him for the test. I explained forgery and its consequences. His grandparents eventually signed.

He was resentful, "They won't let me drive any of their many cars unless I'm running an errand for them. They could let me drive my dad's car; it's just sitting there."

I rationalized, "Maybe they are concerned about insurance. Their insurance might be high because years ago Mr.

Lyonns had a serious accident and hit a child. I think the child died. Their insurance could be higher with a teen-age driver."

He retorted, "The other grandchildren can use their cars or any of the aunts or uncles cars, but I can't use any of them."

Mother was supportive and let him drive her car on a regular basis. To her surprise—and mine when it was relayed to me—Mrs. Lyonns asked, "Why do you let Justin use your car so much?"

"Someone has to show Justin that he can earn trust. I'm showing my vote of confidence by entrusting him with the use of my car."

For some reason, Justin invited his cousin, Randy, into Mother's house when she was gone. There was a long-standing rule that no friends or company were allowed in her home when she was away; permission for exceptions—never granted. To add injury to insult, he took $60. He admitted to taking it.

Mother was livid.

The frequent bowling outings they enjoyed together stopped.

His place of comfort and relief was not available.

He apologized and made a commitment to never betray her trust again. She accepted his apology. Once he got that relationship back on track; Justin never broke her trust or confidence again.

CHAPTER SIXTEEN
Eeny, meeny, miny, mo

> Eeny, meeny, miny, mo
> Catch a tiger by the toe,
> If he hollers let him go.
> Eeny, meeny, miny, mo
>
> —Mother Goose

Summer 1992, Justin came home for three weeks. I told him, "I'm so glad to have you home." In an emphatic tone, Mike expressed the same sentiment. I was glad to see they actively wanted to like each other.

We gave Justin keys to the house and the Nissan truck. He liked the truck; at least, he thought it was a big improvement over the Green Pea. It was like old times. Our relationship fell into its old pattern of humor and closeness. He confided in me and told me about his girlfriends. I listened, chuckled sometimes and challenged him when he was being chauvinistic. I asked, "Where did you get that thinking?"

Breezily, he would tease me or reply with some silly

quip, "Out of the cabbage patch."

Yet, humor was not a part of the conversation we had one of the days I sat on the edge of his bed talking. He was lying across his twin size waterbed looking out the window. Pensively he offered, "I did something bad."

I quietly queried, "What?"

There was a long pause then he told me, "I tried to do what my dad did."

I knew he meant he tried selling drugs. It saddened me that he thought he knew enough about drug dealing to try doing it. The prospect of my son living that kind of life frightened me. But I knew I had to have a measured response—I was quiet for a long time before offering, "You know that's not going to do anything but cause you more trouble."

"Yeah, I know. I didn't feel comfortable doing it and I won't do it again."

The fact that he confessed and promised not to do it again made me hopeful. I rubbed his shoulders and back to calm him as I was thinking of the situation. Then he said, "I've seen what dealing with drugs has done to my dad and I don't want anything to do with drugs."

"Good. I think that's smart and I'm very, very proud of you."

That discussion had me believe I wouldn't have to worry about that pitfall. Justin would not be a good drug dealer. It was a bottom line fact that drug dealers care more about money than they care about people. Justin was too compassionate.

Those summer weeks were good. Justin drove wherever he wanted and stayed within curfew almost always. We were behaving like a real family for the first time until an innocent accident had him more distraught than I thought necessary.

He was blasting his music in the truck as he headed out to a date. I stood at the entrance watching him leave. I yelled a warning as he backed out the driveway, but he couldn't hear me. He hit a parked car! He internalized it and went to his room sad and hurt saying, "I always mess things up when they are going good for me."

"It was just an accident, Justin. No one was hurt. A car can be fixed. You just have to be careful when you're backing out."

Mike called the insurance company and handled everything. He compassionately told Justin, "Accidents happen."

We wanted him to have freedom to drive around but the bed of the truck was long so we decided to give him the Green Pea to drive after that. He didn't like using it, but at least he had transportation.

Thinking it would be a new adventure, we decided Justin would take a train to Toledo instead of flying. Justin packed slowly when it was time to leave. He visited Sharon on departure day and returned home too late to catch the train to Toledo. He said, "I had to stop and put air in the tire."

I complained, "I'll probably have to buy another ticket."

Mike and I talked to Justin about the importance of being responsible. But it seemed evident to me that Justin was purposefully delaying his return to Toledo. I went to his room and asked, "You don't want to go back, do you?"

"Not really."

"Do you think the Lyonnses will send your belongings to you?"

"Probably not all of them."

"Okay, they've started school here already. If you stay you have to change schools again. I don't know what that would do to your graduation status. I don't know how credits transfer."

He mumbled, "I know."

"Maybe you should go back, start gathering your belongings and at Christmas come back here to stay and start school here in January after the break when everyone is coming back at the same time."

He reluctantly agreed, "Okay."

Maybe he was afraid to say out loud what he really wanted; maybe his pride prevented him from speaking up; or worse, maybe he was afraid I didn't want him back? I simply don't know for sure. But I know this for sure. This is something I saw. I saw that he didn't want to return. Even if I suspected he would change his mind again, I should have kept him with me. This is the choice for which I will never forgive myself. I had a long view and considered a bunch of logical logistical, materialistic reasons for not doing what my heart was telling me.

He called Ms. Lyonns to tell her, "Granny, I missed my train and I can't get another until next week."

She icily replied, "I knew you would do this. I told you to be back on time."

I saw his face fall as I listened to her words. I took the phone. "Ms. Lyonns, I assure you it was an accident. The train schedule won't permit a quicker return. I know he needs to get back to start school on time. He will be there in five days."

I remade the sandwiches and snacks I had packed for his trip. Mike gave him money in case he wanted to buy something. Mike and I walked the train track waving until he was out of sight.

CHAPTER SEVENTEEN

A Diller a Dollar

> A diller, a dollar, a ten o'clock scholar!
> What makes you come so soon?
> You used to come at ten o'clock;
> Now you come at noon
>
> —Mother Goose

Justin spent Thanksgiving Day 1992 at a friend's house. Mother was not an option because she was working. Justin felt bad; so I felt bad. Determined to have a better Christmas, I invited all my original family to our home.

I called to ask, "Have you gotten your things together to come home?"

"I've been thinking about going to night school and regular school so I can graduate on time."

"You're young and it is no big deal if you graduate a year later."

"Ummmmm, I don't want to do that."

"Why don't you come back and finish school in Florida?"

"Will I be delayed graduating?"

"Probably, since I don't know of a program in Florida like the one you described."

"No, I don't want to delay my graduation."

I called my mother, "Do you know why Justin is pushing himself to graduate and not come back home as we planned?"

"He made the choice to leave Florida and he's striving toward something; that's admirable. Justin told me, when someone makes a decision, they should stick to it and see it through."

"I've never heard him speak with that line of reasoning. Did someone else put that in his head?"

I paused, thinking through things I'd said. I recalled, "I made a comment a long time ago about him staying in one place and not running back and forth between families. I wonder if that has anything to do with him saying that?"

"I talked to him. I assure you, he is fine with his decision. Maybe you shouldn't stop him while he is trying to do something positive."

I thought that made sense because I had done a lot of talking about working to graduate and now, he was trying. Maybe Mother was right. But there was another reason. Justin had been working at a restaurant and met a young lady, Darlene.

He told me, "She's smart. She has principles and she's kind."

"I thought there was another girl you liked?"

"Well, I decided I like Darlene the best. Sometimes, I talk to other girls just to be doing something, but she is The One. I arranged my schedule so I work when she works because she is my transportation."

"That's awfully nice of her."

"She also takes me to night school and picks me up. We share food when we go out to eat."

It was clear he really liked her. I advised, "Don't have her do too much for you. So you end up relying on her, or taking gifts from her."

In a matter of fact tone, "Mom, it's a mutual thing. When she has, she gives, when I have, I give."

I still worried about Justin attending night school in the brutal Ohio winters. The Lyonnses had stopped driving him to school.

I bought Justin's airline ticket so that he and Mother were seated together. The day after he arrived, he visited with Sharon. He told me, "She's pregnant and her family isn't giving her anything for Christmas. I think that's cruel."

I took my son shopping for new clothes and he invited Sharon along. Justin had counseled her about not putting up with disrespect from the boy she was dating. She bought the boy a shirt. As always, he remained compassionate and bought her a Christmas gift. Sharon's present to him was a photo of herself.

Later, I asked, "Do you still like Sharon?"

"Yes, but..."

Then I teased, "I remember when you were head over heels over her just a year ago. There could be no other."

He laughed. Or maybe it was just a smile. Sometimes his smile felt so bright to me, it seemed like laughter.

That Christmas was good. My brothers and Justin played basketball at a local park. Justin had organized a bowling outing with all of us but after we ate no one wanted to budge. He coerced saying we were reneging on our promises. That sad face said it all. He finally said, "I'll go alone."

Mother chimed in, "I'll go."

I felt bad for breaking a promise, so I recommitted, "I'm going too."

Eventually everyone went except Mike and Gabrielle. It was more fun than we had imagined. The whole family thanked Justin for cajoling us into going. There was a lot of activity packed into a few short days and after he left, I found a Christmas card that I had intended to give him. I put it away with a birthday and Easter cards I had forgotten to send. I would give it to him the next year.

CHAPTER EIGHTEEN

For Want of a Nail

> For Want of a nail, the shoe was lost
> For want of a shoe the horse was lost,
> For want of a horse the rider was lost,
> For want of a rider the battle was lost,
> For want of a battle the kingdom was lost,
> And all for the want of a horseshoe nail.
>
> —Mother Goose

I had always expected Justin to go to college and reminded him frequently to complete his financial aid forms. "I know I need to do it because Darlene got money. But they're hard to fill out."

After a while, it sounded as if he was procrastinating so I got the forms to complete myself. Then, I understood. I felt bad about telling him to finish the forms. He never could have completed them alone. It made me realize how unsupported and alone he was in Toledo. The simple things I would have gladly done were issues because of the miles that separated us.

One day he called very agitated, "They're talking about you Mom. Please send money."

"I do send money every month."

"Yeah, but they are saying it's not enough."

"Ms. Lyonns hasn't said anything to me. I pay for your books and anything else they tell me about over the maintenance amount we agreed to."

"Aunt Laura is talking about you real bad. Please send Granny more money. It will make my life easier while I'm still here."

"Okay, I don't want to make it bad for you. But you can come home you know."

"I know, I've been thinking about moving out of Granny's house."

"You could go live with my mother, until you finish school."

"Well . . . I don't think I want to do that. She gets excited easily. She gets upset and yells and screams a lot. I think I could go to GiGi's house."

"I don't think that's a good idea because she won't guide you to do your homework. She will let you do whatever you want to do. The best place for you is here."

"No, I don't want to come back until I graduate."

He listened to my encouragement and decided, "I'll stay at Granny's until I get out of school."

As I look back, I wonder if that was yet another mistake. Maybe if he left her house earlier, he wouldn't be mentally and emotionally ridden down? It's hard to know for sure without his input and I would not trust anything the Lyonnses say at this juncture. In the final analysis, it had been my job to raise my child.

Message to the Future

CHAPTER NINETEEN

Rinky-Tattle

> Rinky-tittle, rinky-tattle,
> Rinky-tattle----who?
> Little Tommy Taylor
> Is a rinky-tattle too
>
> —Mother Goose

Spring 1993 brought the usual excitements of Prom and the upcoming graduation. Justin described his outfit and the fact that he was allowed to drive one of the Lyonns' cars for Prom night. I was happy for him but knew I was missing out on one of the most important memories of his life. He spoke about going on visits to colleges, within two months I sent over $500 directly to him in support of that.

Again, he was having problems with some boy in school. I advised him to talk to a counselor. He didn't want to be a tattle-tell. I advised, "You know what happened before when you tried to handle things on your own. Please just tell a counselor in confidence."

"It doesn't work like that Mom. If I tell, people will find out. I just try to avoid him."

He was so concerned about the situation he even asked Mike for advice. Mike reluctantly stepped up saying he should not fight the boy at school. After Justin had laid out the details near the end of the conversation, Mike told him "If all else fails, you have to protect yourself."

I decided to call the high school to tell the counselor about Justin's concerns. After I identified myself, there was a distinct chill in the woman's voice. I asked about Justin's grades. She was polite but curt.

"If he passes all his classes, will he graduate?"

Doubtfully, "It's possible."

"I'm trying to make reservations to fly there."

"Oh, I understand, but I'm sorry I can't tell you any more at this point."

Justin happened to be in the office when I called. He heard the conversation and called that night, "Mom I'm an expert on credits."

We laughed. I said, "I tried to call Sheila in California to get your credits transferred, but I haven't been able to reach anyone."

"Oh, Sheila's daughter lives here now, I'll ask her how to get them transferred."

A few days later he called proudly stating, "The credits are being transferred and I handled it myself."

"Well done! Now just pass your classes."

I had gotten so wrapped up in credits I forgot to tell about the threatening boy. I somehow found out why the receptionist at the school was cold toward me. Justin had told Isabelle, who told others when she got him into the school that he had lived alone for a year! I assume he meant after Angela's death. GiGi came to live with us for a while after Angela's death, but she left in July. I thought through what happened after that. I sent him to basketball camps in the summers. However, from August of 1988 until March of 1990, all my efforts still resulted in a struggle to have consistent adult supervision for him when I went on business trips. I know my concern was evident because the accountant traveling with me commented on how often I called home. I always arranged for nearby sitters, but he begged me not to send him to them because he didn't know them. He didn't like going to my aunt's either because he said she was too critical; but I forced him sometimes. My uncle and I knew my aunt's proclivities toward perfection. Uncle Hugh compassionately agreed to stay at our home sometimes, so Justin could be in his own environment. But he was elderly and he sought the comfort of his home too.

In an attempt to make sure Justin had someone with him when I had to travel for work, I once let his dad come stay with him just so someone would be there. That didn't work because he left in the middle of the night leaving a Machiavellian note saying, "*I had to go buddy. You know you are the only one who understands me. I love you."* That was unacceptable; Justin called me at the hotel upset. Here was a situation where I should have taken control, regardless of what he wanted. He claimed, at fourteen, he was old enough to handle things during my short trips. Obviously, that was not the case if he told Isabelle he had lived alone for a year. He must have felt alone but didn't say anything because I would have made him go to a sitter.

Justin continued to be challenged by the pestering boy. He finally got the courage, along with a friend, to ask the boy, "Do you want to fight me or something?"

The boy hit him. They fought. A crowd gathered. Someone in the crowd kicked the boy. Justin broke his hand. Justin had to go to alternative school.

He had to go to summer session to complete his credits. Ms. Lyonns went to court with him. The boy's family pressed charges demanding $250 for doctor's bills. Ms. Lyonns paid. The judge ordered Justin to attend non-violence classes through July.

I offered to pay Ms. Lyonns back. She said, "No. The judge told me to have Justin work and pay me back. The police might arrest him if he leaves town then returns to Ohio without fulfilling the order."

Justin was ready to come back home. I was ready to pay and have him back immediately. But I remembered how he had flip-flopped so many times about where he wanted to live. He might want to return to Ohio to be with his father one day. Even though I knew Justin was not violent. I encouraged him to fulfill the court order.

"Mom, I don't see why I was seen as the aggressor when the boy has a long history of trouble."

I didn't mention that the court looked at his last school incident as part of the evaluation.

The only bright spot was that he could see Darlene a few more times before she went off to college.

CHAPTER TWENTY

Mother May I?

> Mother May I go out to play?
> No my child, I'm afraid you'll stay.
> Take three baby steps.
>
> —Mother Goose

Somewhere during this period, Justin started saying, "I hate my grandmother."

"Why do you feel that way?"

"Because I try to do everything she asks me to do. I do all I can think of, clean the house, and cars, wash the dishes, wash the windows, do the yard, feed the dogs, everything! But she is never happy; never satisfied. She always throws something negative up in my face."

I thought, maybe that's why he seemed so subservient and not the happy-go-lucky child I once knew. He had basically become a slave. I tried to find a bright side.

"Maybe she is trying to get you to become responsible."

He wasn't buying it. He stopped talking regretfully saying, "You don't understand."

"How do you get along with your grandfather?"

"We get along alright ... He teases me about using his car. He says I can use his car as long as I want if I follow two rules. I can only go around the block. I have to be back in ten minutes. And I can never use Granny's car. Pawpaw grabs me and wrestles around. I don't like that. But, in general he is okay."

I silently wondered if anyone kissed or hugged him.

"You'll be leaving soon, so just hang tough and respect your grandparents.

His Aunt Lisa maintained a friendship with Justin. He said she gave him money sometimes and he confided in her. I was sure she then reported his secrets to her mother. That was how they operated. But if I tried to tell Justin that, he wouldn't see it. He would only see she was helping him. He wouldn't see she was not what she projected. He was as naive as I was at his age. It takes a lifetime of experiences to read people and know they are not always as they project themselves. I left my thoughts on her unsaid. He was such a friendly, caring person; I didn't want to start him down my cynical path about how people often disappoint.

In another phone call, Justin said, "They want me to get a job and start working. Uncle Karl sent someone he knows to the house to talk me into a job."

It seemed odd that the Lyonnses encouraged Justin in

that direction when it seemed they encouraged the other grandchildren toward college. I reiterated, "I envision a different future for you. College life is a lot more fun than working a regular job. You have plenty of time to do that. If you do your schoolwork, college life will give you an opportunity to grow, but delay some of the responsibility that comes along with adult life. You will be more likely to find better employment with a college degree and not have to do manual labor if you don't want to."

"You're right; my cousins are in college. I want to go too."

In preparation for his arrival, I enrolled Justin into Valencia junior college in Florida.

After two years, he planned to transfer to Florida A&M, to be with Darlene.

In one call he said, "They are saying they're going to keep me here, and if I run away, they will have me locked up."

"That's ridiculous. I retained legal custody and they cannot make you stay there."

It seemed strange that they would try to keep him there but constantly complained about him. Why the threat? What purpose did it serve?

"Granny said I have to stay until the end of June so we can go see the lawyer."

"Why?"

"I don't know."

I called Ms. Lyonns. "Why does Justin need to stay and

see a lawyer?"

"Awww, it's just some paperwork."

Why was this a secretive delay?

Not long after our conversation, I received a letter from an attorney with a signature block for relinquishing temporary custody. It seemed odd. I wanted him back. I signed. For clarity, I notated that I had always retained legal custody.

Message to the Future

CHAPTER TWENTY-ONE

Jack and Jill

Jack and Jill went up the hill to fetch a pail of water
Jack fell down and broke his crown
Jill came tumbling after.

—Mother Goose

Justin told me the heartbreaking story of how he was banned from seeing Darlene. Reportedly, Ms. Tanner had found Darlene sitting on the side of her bed crying one day. She said she and Justin had argued. Darlene wanted to break up with Justin but was afraid to. Ms. Tanner sought help from her old college friend, Karl. This was the same Karl that had colluded with his deceptive police friend in the kidnapping of my son. Karl had publicly humiliated Justin by accusing him of stealing from his restaurant. Justin said he belittled him and physically threatened him. In his distress, he said, "I feel like killing myself."

From across the miles, I talked him through his anxiety

and humiliation. I did the best I could, but I needed him to have someone who cared about him to give me a first-hand evaluation. I called my mother. I asked her to get Justin and talk to him. He didn't want to discuss anything with her. But I was told Darlene and Justin rendezvoused at GiGi's house every afternoon.

Justin was upbeat when he told me, "I found a summer job through an employment agency."

I could hear he was proud to have done it on his own. I matched his excitement, "I knew you could do whatever you put your mind to do!"

"Granny is telling me to give her my entire paycheck."

"That doesn't sound right."

"I give her some of the money to pay her back for the court payment she made."

"That sounds fair."

Adamantly, "I'm not giving her my entire paycheck."

"I agree, partial payments make sense and sound fair."

Near the end of his time in Toledo, Justin called one morning again asking, "Please send Granny some money because it will make my life easier while I'm still here."

I was surprised because I had paid the Lyonnses consistently each month and he had only two or three weeks before he would be leaving.

"Your aunt called and asked that I contribute to a graduation party for you and your cousin Todd. I committed to $250. I'm not sure I can do a lot more."

Later that day, Justin called me at work saying, "I didn't go to work today because I was sick. My grandmother came into my room and saw me in the bed. She became very, very upset. She began yelling and screaming that I had to go. I had to get up and get out to work. I didn't have transportation so I got on a bike and rode to the job. It was too late, they gave the job to someone else."

"Oh no, . . . it's difficult to find a job."

"Don't worry Mom, I'll find another one. Granny told me I had to leave her house."

I was shocked. There was a long silence.

"I asked her if I could stay for a couple of weeks and she said okay."

I thought everything would blow over until he finished his program at the end of July and then come home.

I again called Mother asking for her assistance. She said, "The chemicals or cleaning agents used on the job irritated Justin's stomach."

That sounded plausible, Justin had complained of stomach irritation off and on for years. I had taken him to several doctors, but none of them ever found anything.

Justin toughed it out through the non-violence program. Somewhere during this time frame, the Lyonnses kicked him out of their house. I continued to call to check on him for a week after he lost his job but he was never home, or I got the voice message or no answer. After about a week, his young cousin, Ryan, answered and told me he didn't live there anymore; he was at GiGi's house. Maybe I shouldn't have been shocked, but I was. He hadn't told me; neither had Ms. Lyonns [who I expected to tell me because I had left him in her care], GiGi nor Mother had told me. Why? Did Justin ask them not to? It dawned on me; maybe this was why it was important for the Lyonnses to sign away temporary custody. It had been a brewing plan to kick him out but they didn't tell me, even when I asked.

When I spoke with Justin, he resentfully offered, "I just don't like my grandmother."

He explained it happened not long after he lost his job. She told him to get out.

"You need to come home."

"I'm ready."

We started making plans for his return. Even though I never thought he had a violent bone in his body, and maybe it was unwise, but I had him finish the last week of the nonviolent program, I thought it was the right thing to do. In my practical way of thinking, I decided in three weeks we would meet in Atlanta for my brother Nick's wedding. He would ride with Mother to Atlanta; after the wedding we would bring him home. He stayed with GiGi.

Mother told me, "Justin called me the day the Lyonnses kicked him out. I was getting ready for work when he called and asked for help. I drove over to the Lyonns 's house and helped him pick up his clothing and other possessions. He looked totally humiliated. His young cousin Ryan compassionately helped him move his things out of the house. His little feelings were hurt to the core and you could see it in his face."

Mother went on to say, "Laura was there. She said Justin was just too disrespectful and none of the Lyonns's children had disrespected her parents so Justin couldn't do it either. Both Ms. Lyonns and Laura said Justin could visit but he could not live there anymore."

It was my fault.

Years ago, two other girlfriends and I sat on the front steps talking about the fathers we had mistakenly chosen for our children. The other two said they didn't care to have the men with whom they chose to have children in their child's life anymore. I asked, "What about male guidance, we can't teach them how to be men." One said, "My brothers and father will fill that role."

The other said, "I'll manage, and Brett will step up when I need him."

I said, "I didn't have Justin alone and I shouldn't have to raise him alone." Their sons still live. I'm not sure if it's the lifestyle they dreamed of for them, but they are alive.

In part, I know I wanted Justin to have his father in his life because my father had opted out of mine. That decision was intended to be for Justin's good. However good principles need good people to carry them out. Justin valued his father. It's likely John manipulated his heart and mind early. He told Justin about his birth and said that I didn't want him but he always did. Justin was young when he told me what John had said. I tried to explain, but large concepts and history are complicated, or I was just inept at presenting them. I thought he was too young to go into adult details, but I did tell him I did not want to have him without being married and that his dad had backed out of our first planned wedding. I said once I held him in my arms, he belonged to me and I loved him.

He became fiercely loyal to his father. I knew I showed Justin love every day and he relied on me for the essentials in life, so I didn't dwell on it. Somewhere along the way, it had become very, very important for Justin to be part of the Lyonns family. I suppose John encouraged that frame of mind. We had our own large, respectable family that showed him love everyday so there was no need to overly value the Lyonnses. Maybe he saw they had more things. I can't know for sure why. I do know that while the Lyonnses had developed a distaste for me, I still believed they had readily accepted and embraced Justin. They were very clannish so I thought they would care for and love him as I could clearly see they did their other grandchildren. Maybe they tried?

GiGi accepted John's collect calls from prison to appease Justin. She ended up with a large bill. She eventually complained to me about Justin running up her phone bill. I told her she shouldn't have accepted so many calls from the prison. She said Justin wanted her to. I knew she would give in to whatever he wanted; I just paid the bill.

Before leaving town, Justin wanted to see his dad one last time. Mother let him use her car to travel to the prison. I'm not sure how he got into the prison alone, since he was only seventeen. Maybe he met up with Mr. Lyonns or one of the other adults or maybe the prison relaxed their rule. Mother told me he was very disturbed when he came back. When she asked what was wrong, he said his chest hurt, but he would work it out. She said, "I didn't push him further for an answer but it was obvious he was bothered."

Much later I found out why he was upset.

We all met in Atlanta for Nick's August 21st wedding. Each morning, Justin picked up Gabrielle to eat the hotel breakfast with him. Then, he took Gabrielle around to other family rooms. One morning, Joe asked why we didn't take Justin shopping with us the day before. I told him Justin always thought that was boring. Justin just looked but did not say anything. Looking back, I see missed opportunities; assumptions; miscommunication.

Friday evening, we dined out and I had vegetables and herbal tea. Justin saw my plate, and compassionately walked over from where he and Joe were seated. He offered me some of his food. It was a challenge to convince him I was okay with what I ordered. So sweet, always genuinely concerned for others, he hugged me tight. Back in the room, he said, "Mom I'm so sorry for missing your birthday. I have something for you."

I unwrapped the present to find a tricolor necklace and earring set.

"Oh I love it!" I said, as I put them on.

"Darlene helped me pick them out."

I gave him a kiss and a hug reiterating how much I liked them.

Nick had a bachelor party at a nightclub. Justin desperately wanted to go, proposing he use a fake identification. I insisted he was too young. Once we got that settled, he was still sullen and felt left out. As a consolation Mother let him drive her car that night. The next day at the wedding, he kept up that old jokester habit. We took family photos and at the end of the shoot, he said, "I wasn't in the family picture."

I panicked, looked around for the photographer and started toward him to tell him he had to do it over.

Justin called me back, "Mom, mom I was in the picture!"

He had that Justin smile on his face. I looked at my youngest brother, Joe; he was nodding and smiling in affirmation.

At the reception we stood together watching everyone. I asked, "Who is that girl you were talking to?"

"She's a student at one of the colleges. She's majoring in respiratory therapy. I told her I was twenty one."

I looked at him and exclaimed, "Justin!"

He gave me a smile and in a hushed tone said, "Quiet mom."

"Why didn't you wear a suit to the wedding?"

"Joe didn't have a suit so we decided to wear matching outfits. I wanted Joe to feel comfortable."

Mike, Gabrielle and I left after an hour or so. Justin wanted to stay and socialize with the family.

Message to the Future

CHAPTER TWENTY-TWO

Three Blind Mice

> Three blind mice, three blind mice
> See how they run, see how they run!
> They all ran after the farmer's wife
> She cut off their tails with a carving knife
> Did you ever see such a sight in your life
> As three blind mice?
>
> —Mother Goose

There was a snag when we moved Justin's luggage from Mother's car to ours. Mike said, "Everything would not fit. There are too many things being stuffed in the car. There isn't enough room for all Justin's things."

Red steam blew from my eyes and ears! I called Mike aside and asked to speak with him privately. Through clenched teeth in a strong soft voice, I made clear, "I WILL NOT ALLOW YOU TO MAKE JUSTIN FEEL BAD."

He defended, "I didn't do anything wrong. I didn't mean

any harm."

I looked at him solemnly and said, "Just don't say ANYTHING negative."

"I want to try to explain."

So, he went down to the car and told Justin he didn't know that he was coming home with us.

When I heard what he said, I was so upset my ears burned fire. I asked him, "What did you think you were doing a few days ago when you carried Justin's boxes into the garage?" I gave him a look of disgust and the evilest look I could conjure up.

I went back down to the parking lot and said, "You know how Mike is. He is so particular about things being a particular way. Don't worry about what he said."

Resigned, Justin said, "I just don't want to cause anyone any trouble."

It hurt me to hear the words and angered me to think Mike, a grown man, had caused the discomfort. He walked to the trunk trying hard to get all his things in the trunk. I said I would sit in the back with boxes stacked around me and on the floor under Gabrielle's car seat; still one box would not fit. He finally said, "it all fit in Granny's trunk and her car is smaller."

We decided to ship one box. Nick volunteered to ship it to us. Justin wasn't comfortable with leaving the box. I said, "It will work out. If the box doesn't come in a week, we'll drive back and get it."

That seemed to make him feel better.

Mike tried explaining again, "I just didn't want us to be uncomfortable with the car stuffed."

I huffily retorted, "You're driving and unaffected—if I don't mind, why should you?"

"I shouldn't."

I watched my son from the backseat as we rode home. He seemed too thin. I made a mental commitment to work on that when we got home. We stopped at a shopping center and Mike bought Justin a lovely, blue silk shirt. The color was perfect for Justin. Yet, it was true, he looked good in every color. He was so handsome.

My family was finally together again and I wanted everything to be right. We gave him a key to the house again and the Green Pea to drive. Mike and I both promised to help him buy a car if he contributed 10% of the cost. At some point, he would get a job. I took him to the campus to register for his classes. With his room reclaimed and school roles defined, we began to settle into a new routine.

Mike became supportive of Justin when he returned home. I could tell he was working toward establishing a better relationship with my son. Each week, Mike filled the Green Pea's gas tank and gave Justin twenty dollars for pocket money.

The first time Mike gave him the money, Justin said, "I'll pay you back."

Mike explained, "No, that's just part of caring for you

and being supportive of you while you're getting through school. You're not expected to pay that back."

It was sad that Justin thought he had to pay for everything. Such a change in two years ... He had been accustomed to being cared for most of his life; he no longer expected that comfort. I hoped to get him to see that he didn't have to pay us back or feel obligated for every little thing.

Justin started his junior college classes. He seemed proud of himself for making it over the hurdles into college. He told me, "My grandmother told me to call when I was enrolled in school."

So, he proudly called to tell her he was in college on Tuesday, August 24, 1993.

He spent a lot of time in our home office on the computer. He often wrote letters to Darlene and his dad. He shared parts of his letters to Darlene but he never shared any of his letters to his dad. He received two letters from Darlene, but none from his dad. Intuition told me to open the last letter he asked me to mail to his dad. I rationalized that little voice away by saying I should honor his privacy.

Saturday, August 28, he drove to Tallahassee to see Darlene. He told me he was going to give Darlene an engagement ring. I didn't approve. Mike gave him directions and a map. He also gave him money for gas and tolls. At the last minute, Mike walked out and gave Justin our AAA card, just in case of an emergency. He also gave him the car phone and radar detector. "Call if you have any problems."

I chimed in, "And call to let us know you got there safely. And, don't make a lot of long distance calls."

He was smiling as he backed out of the driveway. I waved and watched until I couldn't see the car anymore. I thought, *This is the way it's supposed to be. He's growing up. I'm going to lose him to adulthood soon.*

He came home tired Sunday. He immediately went to bed. Later in the day, he got up and worked on the computer. I expected him to be happy. He wasn't. I asked, "How was your trip?"

"It was okay."

"Where did you sleep?"

"In the car. The plan Darlene and I made was messed up."

I suspected he thought he could stay in the dorm, but I didn't ask about that.

"Why didn't you call home?

"I did but I got the answering machine and didn't leave a message. I psyched someone into letting me shower in a hotel room this morning. I talked to Darlene then headed home."

I hoped Justin would start dating other girls.

"When we were on campus I saw a real, real pretty girl. Did you notice her?"

"No, where did you see her?"

"In the bookstore."

"I must not have been around."

I thought, *At least he asked about the girl*. Then he asked, "Can Darlene and I sleep in the same room if she comes to visit?"

I chuckled, "No, she can sleep in the guest room and you can sleep in another room."

Later that day Justin was walking behind me and said, "You're about the same height as Darlene."

I didn't comment.

Then nostalgically he asked, "Do you remember how it was when just you and I lived together?"

The tone in his voice was sentimental and nostalgic of something lost. I observed, "You sound as if we were lovers."

He didn't say anymore. I had missed his point about loving a certain time in our lives. I didn't sync up with his thinking.

Conversations on the phone and a few visits throughout the year had me with an incomplete picture of who my child had become. My thoughts and reactions remained rooted in the many phases of our relationship before he left.

Gabrielle became sick. Mike took her to his mother's house so we wouldn't have to miss work. Just the three of us returned to our weekly routine. We ate dinner and watched TV together. Justin talked on the telephone and worked or played on the computer. I reminded him to study. The next night he surprised us with dinner. He made a chicken dish similar to the one I had prepared the night before. I smiled to myself thinking, *He must have really liked dinner last night*. Also, it was obvious he was trying to make things pleasant. He reached for both our hands when we started to bless the food. I glanced at Mike. It was a huge surprise. Before he left Florida, he refused to hold hands during grace. Justin added a few words of prayer after Mike finished saying grace. It was so thoughtful and sweet.

The bliss was interrupted as we settled into our evening routine. Ms. Lyonns called and accused Justin of stealing a check from her. She said, "You wrote a check to yourself for $200 and cashed it."

We all listened to her on the speaker phone and it was clear she was livid. She yelled, "Justin, don't lie. I know your writing and your driver's license number was written on the check!"

Justin quietly responded, "I didn't do it."

Ms. Lyonns hotly replied, "I will investigate further and check the driver's license number! Mary Lou call me back after ten a.m. tomorrow morning."

I agreed and we hung up.

After we hung up, I chastised Justin saying, "If you did it, I think it is detestable and awful that someone with their health and strength would take money from his or her grandmother. People who are healthy should work for what they want. I work every day and it's not as if it's some great joy, but it is necessary, and if I work every one in the house should work."

I paused and said, "We'll wait to see what she finds before we discuss it further. Justin went to his room. Mike asked to me come into the front room.

He said, "Take it easy on him. You said you were going to wait to see what happens. If you're actually going to wait until she gets more information, then do so."

Regretfully I asked, "Did I say the wrong thing?"

"No but your voice sounded irritated and accusatory."

I went to Justin's room. He was sobbing. Through tears of pain he said, "I can never get away from it. There were other times when Granny accused me and when she found out she was wrong, she never apologized."

I calmly soothed, "I heard that complaint from other children in that family. What she typically does is try to make up for wrong accusations by buying you something nice. There have been other occurrences of missing money in the Lyonns's household long before you were born. It will be okay. You haven't done anything to us and that is all that matters. If you've left that type behavior behind, we don't have a problem. We trust you based on how you are with us."

Justin was literally standing in a corner with his back against the wall. His cassette tapes were on the floor in front of him. I squeezed into the narrow space, put my arms around him and said, "It will be okay. We'll find out what she says tomorrow." I gave him a little squeeze and tried to calm him down.

CHAPTER TWENTY-THREE

The Bells

"You owe me five shillings," Say the bells of St. Helen's.
"When will you pay me?" Say the bells of Old Bailey.
"When I grow rich," Say the bells of Shoreditch.
"When will that be?" Say the bells of Stepney.
"I do not know," Says the great Bell of Bow.

—Mother Goose

1 September 1993

I didn't call Ms. Lyonns the next day. In fact, I dreaded ever hearing from her again. When I got home, I started fixing dinner and asked Justin if he would go to the store for an onion. When Justin went outside, he told Mike he was too dizzy. Mike sent him back inside and he went directly to his room. Mike came in and said, "Justin doesn't look good."

It took a few minutes to get the food to a point of simmer, then I went in to talk to him. I sat on the floor next to his bed and asked, "What is wrong?"

He started crying softly, "I want to go to the hospital."

"Why, do you feel that bad?"

"Mom, I did something."

"What?"

He was silent a long, long time. I looked around and saw a glass on the night-stand and two open bottles of pills. One was Tylenol, the other was an ulcer medication. I had forgotten about them and had been carrying them in my purse for over a week. I'd only recently given them to him. Not all the pills were gone, but most were. "Did you take these pills?"

"Yes."

My mind reeled back to the time in my early teen years—maybe thirteen or fourteen—when I was overwhelmed with all the work of cleaning the house and being responsible for my siblings, maintaining good grades, trying to fit in somewhere, trying to understand life and being impoverished with no way out; I just wanted to end my life. I had sat on my mother's green, tweed sofa with the Spanish-style wooden adornments on its back. White- sheer curtains covered the picture window to my right and swung in the breeze. A picture of a running brook with trees lining a small hill hung on the wall behind me. I had cleaned up and the living room was neat as could be. I sat with a glass of water and all the medication I could find in the house. It was some sort of aspirin type medication and one by one I put them in my mouth and swallowed. I sat for a long time in the rarely quiet house with full intent to leave this earth. Before I could finish, someone came home and I hurriedly hid the medication and went to bed. I woke up the next day and life continued. I never told anyone. Not even my beloved Angela.

I wondered what was so bad that he wanted to kill himself. We weren't poor. If it was his grandmother, all he had to do was promise to repay. Had I missed something?

I asked, "Why?"

I waited a long time then asked, "Do you want to tell me why?"

Another long pause before he mumbled, "I'll talk later."

I tried to convince in a matter of fact tone that ended in a plea, "Justin you have a lot to live for, please don't do that to yourself anymore."

I got off the floor and asked, "Can you get up to eat?"

"No leave some out for me, I'll eat later."

"Can you drink some water?"

"No."

I left and come back with apple juice. "Here's some apple juice, I want you to drink it."

I stood there a long time looking at him until he finally drank it.

I went to check on the meal I was cooking and went back to Justin's room with more juice and a plum. "Please drink a little more."

He sipped a bit and promised, "I'll drink the rest later."

I emptied the trash can and put it next to his bed in case

he needed to throw up.

I thought I would call Mother to find out if the medication was harmful.

I finished cooking and Mike and I sat to eat. He asked, "Is Justin going to join us?"

Distracted, I said, "No, he's not feeling well."

I sat thinking, eating, and wondering what to do. I finally shared, "he tried to do something harmful."

"Like what?"

"Well, he took some pills and I'm still trying to decide what to do about it."

Mike was silent.

As usual I rationalized and second-guessed my gut feelings. I started thinking, *I got through a depressed patch, he'll get over this depressed feeling too. Maybe I should take him to the hospital? The emergency room will likely take forever. They will likely charge an arm and leg for nothing. He's conscious. I don't think they pump a person's stomach if they are conscious? I don't know what to do.*

If only I had just considered the emotional burden he was under. I didn't know is not an acceptable excuse. It was my responsibility to know. I had signs he was more self-conscious about little things but I had let a bad-behaving, confident, mentally and physically well person leave me. I thought I had gotten a similar maturing person back. If only I had taken him to the hospital, or called Mother, maybe someone could see what I couldn't. I didn't think of any of that—I had a longer view—everything would work itself out. I got up from the table to check on him. He had finished the apple juice.

"Do you want to talk now?"

"Not now, later."

2 September 1993

I went to the kitchen to look for evidence Justin had eaten something and found he had at least eaten a piece of chicken. I thought, *That's a good sign.*

I knocked at his door and heard a mumble. I went in to check on him. He turned to look at me from his bed. His eyes were slits. They were filled with hurt. I thought, *this must be about Ms. Lyonns accusation.*

I asked, "Justin why did you take the pills?"

"I don't feel like talking now."

I didn't want to pressure him. I decided to wait until he was ready to talk. I closed his door and left for work.

When I called Justin to see if he would make it to his Thursday classes, he was preparing for school. He called back later to ask if there was anything that I wanted him to do. It was a newly developed habit and he didn't have that free-to-just-be attitude I had known him to have. He was unhappy before he left Florida but this was different. I didn't understand it but I guessed he was just maturing. I had to think hard to find something for him to do. I suggested, wipe off the counter, let some water out of the pool and vacuum.

He said, "I can do everything except vacuum because I have to get back to class." I didn't care, I had just thought of things that could be done not things that were needed. Then he said, "I can come have lunch with you."

"That would be nice, but I already had lunch. Maybe you can come over next week and we can have lunch together."

"Okay."

I made the dreaded call to Ms. Lyonns. She huffily explained, "The girl at the credit union felt sure it was Justin who cashed the check. "

I asked her a lot of questions not wanting to believe but trying to make sure she was right. I told Mike. We agreed, we had to have a talk with Justin.

Justin came home later than usual that night. He went to the family room and sat on the couch to watch TV.

Mike started, "Our neighbor down the street works at Disney World, he said he would get you a job there."

He replied, "Disney World is a long way from home."

I confirmed his comments with, "I agree."

Mike continued, "There could be other benefits to working at Disney, like . . meeting girls"

Justin flashed that signature smile and said, "I might have been interested a year ago, but not now. I'm dedicated to Darlene. I don't think I'll take the job at Disney because it will use up a lot of gas and time traveling there."

I spoke up from the kitchen table saying, "Come over here so we can talk."

He turned the TV off and sat across from me with his head slightly cocked.

"I spoke to your grandmother today and she said your Aunt Lisa told her that you said you wrote the check."

Justin admitted, "I spoke with her and she said something quickly and I just said yeah."

My voice was a pitch higher when I queried, "You don't know what she said?"

Self-consciously, "No."

I continued in the same tone, "Do you know that's how police get confessions out of people?"

I repeated his grandmother's comments, "She said she didn't know what happened to the $500 Kerry gave you for graduation. She said she only knew you bought shoes and a shirt and she said Kerry felt bad you left without saying goodbye to him."

Justin didn't say anything. He sat looking down at the table.

"She said you have thirty days to get the money back before she signs papers to prosecute you."

I lowered my voice, paused and matter-of-factly said, "You need to get a job. You'll be eighteen in a few weeks and I won't be able to protect you anymore. You'll be accountable and responsible for your actions. We don't mind paying for your school things and gas, but if you want other things, you have to work. You have to work in school also. We will pay for everything but we can't afford to do that if you won't do your best. I'm not sure you're studying enough."

Justin raised his head and looked at me for a moment. At that moment, I started to say, *'but I'll always be here to help you if you help yourself.'* That was my heart telling me what to say, but my head thought it would dilute the points I was trying to make. I thought, *maybe that was the problem, I'd been too soft with him.* I decided, *I'll tell him that tomorrow.*

The family room and kitchen were open to each other and Mike was at the edge of the family room ironing his shirt. In a calm voice, he offered, "If you did it, we just want you to face it and work out some sort of payment plan. I believe your grandmother just wants you to do the right thing. I think that will take care of the problem. Then you can put this behind you and go on."

I added, "Then you can be done with it."

Justin responded, "I'm only going to be here a year, then I'm going to school and not have any contact with my family."

I immediately thought that was different from yesterday. He had said he would be here two years, complete his associates degree and transfer to Florida A&M. Who was he talking about? His dad? The Lyonnses? My family? Did he mean me? Did he not want contact with me?

I rejoined the conversation, "Why don't you want any contact with your family?"

"I just think it's best."

Mike asked, "Don't you think that would be painful? Your family will be the ones who stand beside you in your hardest times. You can't afford to alienate those who you love and who love you, like your grandmother. Your mother, and whether you believe it or not, I am your best ally in this. We want to see you face it and go beyond this point."

Almost simultaneously we asked, "Did you take the check?"

Justin tightly stated, "I'd like to work this out with my grandmother and not say any more about it tonight."

I saw the stress in his face. My heart wrenched. I wanted to give him relief. I said, "Okay."

Mike started, "We want to get this behind you."

Justin stood and started walking toward his room. Tears of pain were in his face. As he walked, he responded, "My mom ... [long pause] I'll work it out with my grandmother."

I glanced at Mike and he said, "Okay."

As he left, I watched the narrow heel of his foot in the house slippers we had bought on a trip to Hawaii. The image was etched in my brain.

After a while, Justin went into the office to work on the computer. He sat in the black, high-backed, leather chair facing the computer when I walked into the room. I sat on the arm of the red leather sofa to be close to him. I knew he felt bad, so I didn't know how to start the conversation. Then I heard myself saying, "You can get this behind you and go on."

In a resigned voice, Justin said, "I'll never be able to live it down. Just because I've done things in the past, I can never get rid of them."

"Yes, you can."

Justin's toned changed, "Now come on, Mom, did you seriously never think I'd do something or steal something?"

I truthfully replied, "I can't say I haven't thought about it, but we made a decision to trust you unless you showed us otherwise. You haven't done anything to break our trust so we don't have a problem."

In a strained voice, "I feel like killing myself and I'm just going to keep trying until I do. I see why people kill themselves, it's so much pressure."

I asked, "What kind of pressure?"

"Just pressure. I had this book about suicide."

"I remember it."

"Read that book. It talks all about it."

"Where is it?"

"In Ohio somewhere."

Almost pleading and chastising at once, "Justin, don't talk like that. I want you to do well in life. One of the last things I told Angela before she died was to fight; I want you to do that."

"I know what you're trying to do. You're trying to psyche me out."

Defensively I said, "No. I'm not! I'm tired and I'm sleepy. I'm not playing any games. I'm telling you what I feel."

It was after 1:00 a.m. when I went to our bedroom. I prepared for bed but couldn't lie down. I thought Mike would have the words to appeal to him. I asked, "Will you please speak to Justin about the Saturday seminar for young, Black males at the Expo Center?"

Mike started the conversation with, "We want you to pick up some products for delivery tomorrow. I've filled the truck with gas and I'm leaving the key, a blank check and directions on how to get to the facility. I'll pay you to run this errand. Justin responded, "No, I don't have to pay you for things you do for me."

Our bedroom was close to the office. Mike came into the bedroom and told me what was said. We chuckled that he didn't want to get paid when we knew he needed to get his financial footing. Mike left again to convince Justin to attend the Saturday event. Justin had gone to his bedroom.

I couldn't relax. I wanted to be sure the conversation was all positive so I stood in the hallway out of sight and listened to them talk. He showed Justin the flyer and explained, "This is for high risk teenagers but there will also be people talking about job opportunities. I know some of the people organizing it and they are good people. It's going to emphasize how young people can see the positive potentials in life."

Justin listened with his face down on his bed and said, "I'll think about it. Can you leave the flyer so I can read it?"

Mike left the flyer on the dresser.

When I woke up the next day, I had no idea it would be the worst day of my life.

I looked at the directions Mike had written. I told him, "These are confusing. Justin knows even less about Orlando than I do."

"I know. They're incomplete. I'll call him and finalize them about ten this morning."

I repeatedly called Justin and got no answer. My first impulse was to go home, but Mike had the car. I called Mike and left a message asking for the car. He called back and complained, "We're relying on Justin and he can't be found. I don't know how I can get the car to you now. I have an important meeting so I can't spend any more time on this now. I'll call you back."

I had a feeling of dread. As usual I rationalized. I convinced myself Justin had gone to see Darlene. I calculated he would arrive in Tallahassee about 3:00, if he left after we hung up. At 3:30, I called Darlene. Her answering machine picked up. I left a message asking her to call me back collect.

Message to the Future

Part II

Message to the Future

CHAPTER TWENTY-FOUR

Ring Around the Roses

> Ring around the roses, a pocketful of posies,
> Ashes! Ashes! We all fall down
>
> —Mother Goose

I was wrong about his intentions. After an exhausting night of dealing with death, I woke up at Mrs. Lamm's house frantic to get to Tallahassee. I wanted to see and speak with Darlene to see if she knew more about Justin's state of mind. GiGi called Mrs. Lamm's house early in the morning to give Mother's flight number and arrival time. Then she offered, "Uhhh ... by the way, I spoke to Mrs. Tanner and she said Justin and Darlene broke up. They don't want anyone to tell their daughter about Justin's death over the phone. Mr. Tanner is flying out this morning. He wants to meet with Darlene and tell her personally. Uhh ... they also said they don't want you to see Darlene."

I resented the fact that GiGi had told Darlene's parents so much so quickly and they were going to make it difficult for me to speak to Darlene at all. I needed to get there right away!

Mike picked up mother from the airport but he didn't come back until three o'clock in the afternoon! The day was getting away from us and I needed to get to Tallahassee. I paced and cried and cried and paced. Finally, I decided to go to the bus station when Mike drove up. My mother walked into the house and looked at me with eyes that belied a broken heart. She gave me a long hug as if she was trying to drain the pain away from me and soak it into her body. I turned to Mike and in a tearful voice I insisted, "We've got to go! We have to go to Tallahassee to see Darlene right away because the Tanners are going to stop me from speaking to their daughter."

Mike looked puzzled. He envisioned me talking with my mother and getting much needed comfort. In my frenzy, Mother, Mike and I hurried to the car. I lamented, "It will be night before we arrive. We should fly. We rushed to the airport.

Mike was at the ticket counter and I used the airport phone booth to call Mrs. Tanner. At the sound of my voice she offered condolences. Then in a don't-you-know tone she stated, "Justin and Darlene broke up but Justin has been calling, yelling and screaming at Darlene."

As I stood there listening, my heart dropped. It didn't

seem like something Justin would do, but maybe this was an area of his life I didn't know very well, so I listened as Mrs. Tanner continued, "Darlene and her roommate changed the phone message in an effort to get him to stop."

I asked, "Which dorm is Darlene in?"

She declined to say but continued on about Darlene, problems with their relationship, why her husband was traveling without her and distinct distancing of herself and her family from Justin ... It was clear she resented him.

It all felt like a heavy weight on me. Mike walked up with the tickets we bought and stood next to me. I handed the phone to him and plopped down in a nearby seat. I heard him asking Mrs. Tanner, "Try to understand ... have a little compassion."

I discovered the flights wouldn't get us there until the next day—not soon enough so we returned the tickets and decided again to drive.

It was dark when we finally reached the campus. I dialed Darlene's number and got no answer. It was clear we had to stay overnight to see Darlene; we checked into the Radisson across from the campus entrance. Mike called Mrs. Tanner saying we would see Darlene tomorrow. A few minutes later, Mr. Tanner called the room saying in a formal, nasally voice, "I'm sorry to hear about what happened. I can meet you in the hotel lobby shortly. I'll be there at one o'clock."

When I hung up the phone, mother protectively warned me, "It might be an unpleasant meeting."

"I know, Mom, but I have to give it a chance."

I could tell she was worried about me. She had flown several hours, then I'd whisked her off with me on a long drive. I figured she had to be tired after a tension-filled day.

Mr. Tanner promptly showed up in the lobby at 1:00 a.m. I watched his slim, six-foot frame lightly bounce across the room in his tasseled, black leather loafers. His close-cropped, wrinkly hair was speckled with gray. He wore an argyle vest over a black turtleneck and black, cuffed, khaki pants. Next to him was a muscular man who he introduced as his cousin. The man strangely called him Mr. Toner; I had my doubts about the relationship.

Mike and I guided Mr. Tanner and his "cousin" to a secluded corner of the lobby where there was a small sofa covered in fabric with a tiny rose pattern. In front of it was an oval-shaped, dark, highly polished wooden coffee table, with an intricately carved design along the two-inch, high edges. Flanking the sofa were two cloth-covered, wing-backed chairs with a small diamond print. Mike and I sat on the sofa.

As anticipated, Mr. Tanner was protective of his daughter. He had incorrectly decided I would blame her for Justin's death. We attempted to get his permission to speak with his daughter in his presence. I started, "I understand you want to protect Darlene, but I mean her no harm. I just want to ask her a few questions."

He said no. He blinked hard several times then hotly

retorted, "You didn't know what was going on with your son. I could tell you a lot."

Not having the mental acuity to ask for more information, I defended, "I spoke to him every day. I knew Justin talked to you and liked you."

"That doesn't matter. There was a lot you didn't know. I offered Justin a job and he didn't take it."

"He got a job on his own."

"But I offered him a better job and he wouldn't take it."

"I just want to have a short conversation with her. It would help me"

"My daughter has nothing to do with this. What you want doesn't matter. You made your choices, now this is what you have."

I couldn't hold back the tears, so I left the lobby. I got to the door of our room and turned around. I couldn't leave this up to Mike. It was my child we were talking about. I rode the elevator back to the lobby. I sat next to Mike as he was championing my position. I started to say something, but Mr. Tanner turned his wire framed professorial looking face to me and said, "I'd rather talk to him."

I was stunned. Mike turned and looked at me, seeing I was devastated by Mr. Tanner's words. He turned back to Mr. Tanner and in a calm come-on-now voice implored, "Have a little compassion."

Mr. Tanner hesitated before replying, "You're right."

After a brief pause, Mr. Tanner continued in his high-handed voice, "I understand how you feel, but no conversation can bring your son back."

Mike spoke up, "You couldn't understand how she feels unless you have lost a child."

For the first time, the distant cousin spoke in a deep rumbling voice, "I know what it feels like. I had a son who was healthy and strong one day and then he was gone."

We all looked surprised. Mike asked, "Under the same circumstances?"

The muscular distant cousin admitted, "The circumstances were very different. My son was shot by another young man."

We all paused taking that in. I told the man I was sorry for his loss. Then I turned to Mr. Tanner and virtually begged for permission to speak with his daughter.

"No, she will be under too much stress."

I finally suggested, "I live here in Florida. I could do this without your permission because you can't stay here forever. But I don't want to do it that way."

Mr. Tanner concluded the meeting saying, "I will get back in touch in the morning."

As soon as we entered the room my mother asked, "How did the meeting go?"

Mike pondered out loud, "I wonder if the Tanners and others in Toledo played mind games and verbal gymnastics like that with Justin?"

I responded, "I don't know, but I can't imagine how

he would have dealt with such treatment and games of semantics. It was difficult for the two of us and we're adults..."

While the Tanner's approach was insensitive, I knew if the tables were turned, I would have been protective of my child as well. He had a right to try to protect her. We wanted to honor that right and go through them. Even though I said I had no ill intentions, they didn't know I meant their daughter no harm.

I decided to call Mrs. Tanner and plead with her. She was a mother too after all. I implored Mrs. Tanner to reason with her husband. I relayed all that her husband and his distant cousin said, including the statement that they had already told Darlene about Justin's death.

In a surprised voice, Mrs. Tanner said, "I don't see how that can be possible! I don't think he has found Darlene."

Mrs. Tanner went on to say, "I knew Justin was disturbed and violent. I deal with children like him all the time and I could tell he was missing something."

Mrs. Tanner was an attorney for impaired children. She was not speaking of the Justin I knew. He did many things that challenged me, but violence was never a part of his personality. I had not known him to be disturbed, but I could not say for sure what he was like in Toledo when I was not there and I was sad and ashamed of that fact.

The people of Toledo often commented on how much he looked like his dad; who did have a violent streak. Maybe Mrs.

Tanner thought that, since he looked like his dad, he would behave like him also. I didn't want to say anything negative, because I was pleading with her to give me permission to speak with her child. But, as she continued, I finally broke in, raised my voice and defensively stated, "In terms of material things, Justin had just as much or more than your children. I loved him just as you love your children. I know you spoke to Karl Lyonns, your old college buddy, to ask him to stop Justin from contacting Darlene. Karl attacked my defenseless son on your behalf. Justin told me Karl belittled him and physically threatened him. He told me he hated his Uncle Karl and felt like killing himself. So, at this point I just want your assistance. Once I've spoken with her, we will not contact Darlene again unless she contacts us."

Mike came close and asked for the phone and I gave it to him. I could hear him attempting to reason with her, "Please be compassionate and try to understand from a mother's perspective. Think about what you would want if the tables were turned, . . ."

My mother tried to be comforting, but she too was intensely affected by what she was hearing. I knew she hoped for the best; she always wanted the best for me. Before going to bed, Mike and I prayed the Tanners would be merciful.

CHAPTER TWENTY-FIVE

The Lost Shoe

> Doodle doodle doo,
> The Princess lost her shoe:
> Her Highness hopped, -
> The fiddler stopped.
> Not knowing what to do.
>
> —Mother Goose

Sunday, September 5, 1993

Prayer works. The phone rang at 7:45 a.m. Mr. Tanner's overly formal nasal voice started, "Darlene has agreed to..." He stopped. I suspect Darlene was close by because he rephrased his words, softened his tone and said, "Darlene wants to meet you. We will be in the hotel lobby in fifteen minutes." Promptly at 8:00 a.m., Mr. Tanner, the distant cousin, Darlene and a young man came in and we silently escorted them to the private library Mike and the hotel manager had arranged for us to use.

The library was a huge room. When you walked through the double doors and turned to the right, all three walls were filled with rich-looking shelves, holding leather-bound books from floor to ceiling. In the center stood a long, dark, wood conference table that was covered in glass surrounded by twelve red leather chairs. To the left of the double doors there was a sitting area. A long diamond-patterned sofa was stationed beneath a round, stained glass window; another sofa was opposite it. Both sofas were cream colored with some blue in the pattern. A dark, wood, rectangular coffee table was in the center. A foot or two away from each end of the coffee table there were two, large, blue, velvet-looking, wingback chairs.

We all introduced ourselves. Darlene's eyes were very red. I had only seen pictures of her. Justin showed me the prom pictures they took and portraits taken before she went away to college. She was more petite than she looked in the photos. I was surprised at her long, voluminous, chestnut brown hair. It made her large doe-like eyes even more striking; she was a beauty! I thought she and Justin must have been absolutely striking together. Mike and I sat on the sofa beneath the stained glass window. The room echoed with silence. I cleared my throat, sought Darlene's eyes and said, "Darlene, Justin has told me many things about you. I'm grateful for what you did for him. Justin told me you helped and encouraged him when you two worked together. He told me about the rides to work and school and that you shared whatever you had with him. I'm thankful for all your efforts."

I paused, then asked, "Do you know of anything that might have been troubling him?"

Darlene looked at me, "No."

Silence. "Did Justin threaten you or hurt you?"

She hesitated then responded, "No."

Mr. Tanner had been quiet until then. He pointed out, "Those are two separate questions and you should answer each separately."

Darlene reconsidered then replied, "Justin threatened me once, but he never hurt me."

I asked, "Did it happen recently?"

"No, it was some time ago."

The young man who accompanied them was sitting to my left. I could feel his eyes on me. I turned to look at him. He looked away.

I secured eye contact with Darlene and continued, "I promised not to contact you again, but you can contact me if you choose to do so. I will do what I can for you if you need anything. From what I've heard and seen, you have done well in school and you should continue to do so. You are an attractive girl. There will be a lot of young men in your life but it is important to keep your grades up."

When it was clear I was finished, Mr. Tanner stood up and spoke in a cordial, relieved tone, sincerely saying, "I'm sorry about what happened."

Everyone stood. I asked Mr. Tanner, "Is it okay if I hug

Darlene?"

Without hesitation he consented, "Sure, sure."

I embraced Darlene and whispered in her ear, "Are you pregnant?" She nodded her head ever so slightly.

"Call me; we'll work it out."

They left.

Mike tried to console me as we sat in the quiet library with the sun shining brightly through the windows. I felt the emptiness that filled the room and interrupted the silence with my sobbing.

We drove back to Mrs. Lamm's house where they were putting finishing touches on a cake celebrating Gabrielle's two years of life. I stood there and smiled for birthday photos. As soon as I could, I escaped to stand at a large picture window to look into the darkened sky that was pouring down rain. It matched the dark sadness in my heart.

Message to the Future

CHAPTER TWENTY-SIX

What are Heavy?

What are heavy? Sea-sand and sorrow;
What are brief? Today and tomorrow;
What are frail? Spring blossoms and youth;
What are deep? The ocean and truth

—Mother Goose

The carbon monoxide was so bad we had to stay in a hotel for three days. I didn't want to go back into the house. I didn't want to live there anymore but we had sold the condo. I had nowhere else to go.

I had to make arrangements to bury my baby, my son, my first born child. I saw the answering machine blinking when I walked into our office. There were a lot of messages from five of the thirteen members of the Lyonns's family. I heard the voices of Kerry, Maria, Donald and Marcus. Then I heard Laura say she was trying to set up a three-way call with John. At that moment, I knew no matter what I wanted to do, they would take issue with it. I didn't feel like talking but I didn't want to be rude. Marcus and Donald each said they were sorry but John would not be able to attend the funeral unless it was in Toledo. Kerry said, "I'm sorry about Justin. What happened? Did anything happen? Did you argue before he took his life?"

I offered him more words than I had spoken to anyone. I told him about the telephone conversation with his mom and the follow up discussion we had. He said, "I don't know what you are feeling, but I'm sorry. I don't want to pressure you, but I want to ask you to take my brother's ability to attend the funeral and inability to go out of the state of Ohio into consideration."

I felt tiny at that moment. I heard myself say, "I'll consider it. I know John loved Justin. I sometimes did not agree with his parenting, but I know he loved him."

Kerry was quiet for a long time. Then he asked, "Where's Justin's body being held?" I gave him the hospital name, coroner's name and telephone number.

I shakily walked into the kitchen to get water. Mother and Mike were surprised at how shaky I was. They both encouraged me to not return any more calls. I went back to courteously finish what I had started. Maria's message said, "I don't want to pressure you, please call me back." Maria had been at the hospital with me when Justin was born. She had massaged my neck the same way Mike's sister, Cynthia, massaged it at his death. I called her. She offered condolences then said, "I know it's hard to hear right now, but it was all in 'The Plan' from the day Justin was born. The Lord takes care ... etc. My mind couldn't comprehend what she was saying. After her thoughts were out, she paused.

I responded, "You're right."

Then she asked, "What are you doing about the funeral arrangements?"

"They will probably be in Florida."

She replied, "Well, I guess no one can change your mind. I just thought it would be in Toledo since Justin has spent most of his life here and was only in Florida a few months."

My head was spinning; I replied, "He was with me all but a year-and-a-half of his life."

In a tone of incredulity Maria responded, "Mary Lou! Justin came to Toledo in his tenth grade year ... and he graduated from here."

I said, "I'm not going by grades because his credits were messy. We moved into this house in 1991 and Justin was with me then."

Maria went through a long discourse about how long Justin lived with me. She insisted I was wrong about my timeframes. She finally pointed out that June of 1991 to June of 1993 was two years.

Painfully, I agreed.

It was clear Justin's funeral was expected to be in Toledo because we had lived there most of our lives.

I lived there as a child and I spent my early adulthood

years trying to leave for more and better opportunities. He was nine when we left. Those choices had brought me to this painful place in my life. For me, "home" had come to be wherever I was comfortable and happened to be. To make up for the mistake of letting him leave, I decided he would be with me the rest of my life. I would have him cremated and keep his ashes with me in an urn until I died.

Maria continued the conversation, "I heard you called Momma and said Justin wouldn't be paying her back the money because he was dead. You shouldn't blame my mother for what happened."

At that point, I yelled, "If anyone wants to know who to blame, blame me! I am to blame! I was put on this earth to protect him and now he is gone. I am to blame."

Sounding satisfied, she offered, "As a mother, I knew you would say that. You feel you should have been with him. Justin had a hard life."

That was a surprise to me. His life had not been hard with me. Maybe he was lonely sometimes, but certainly not hard. I assumed she was talking about his life in Toledo during his stay. I looked up and my mother and Mike were standing in the door. Mike had his hand out asking for the phone.

I glanced down as I heard Maria say, "A number of people in Ohio want to attend his funeral."

I responded, "If he had killed himself in Ohio, I would have traveled anywhere in the world to attend his funeral.

I'm glad it didn't happen while he was away from me. I guess you're right the Lord must have a plan."

She questioned, "What?"

I repeated myself then said, "Those who loved and cared for him will be at the funeral. They will make a way."

Maria defensively replied, "It's not about money."

I remained quiet. After a while Maria finally said, "Well ... I guess you will give Momma the details."

I stated, "Yes, I will call her. I apologize for getting upset. I hope I didn't say anything to hurt you. Thank you for calling."

Maria ended by murmuring, "I understand. I just thought I should call."

Mike returned Mrs. Lyonns's call to impart funeral arrangements. He said it was difficult getting through to her because she kept asking about the funeral being in Toledo. At some point, Mrs. Lyonns gave the phone to Isabelle. Isabelle reiterated the fact that they wanted the service in Toledo so John could attend his son's funeral. Mike said, "Everyone is welcome to come to Florida and John's inability to attend the funeral was not Mary Lou's doing; it is the state of Ohio's doing."

Isabelle then asked for Justin's body when we were done with it so they could have a service. It hurt to think they were treating Justin's remains as a commodity with little regard for the person who existed.

The conversation ended with Isabelle saying she wanted me to at least call Mrs. Lyonns again. Mike reported, she pointedly said money was not an issue. It had nothing to do with them coming to Florida.

I asked, "Why did money come up?"

Mike said, "I got the impression it was something they had discussed among themselves based on Maria's call."

GiGi said she saw a notice in the paper for a memorial service for Justin. We guessed that meant the Lyonnses would not attend the funeral. It was not the way Justin would have wanted it. When he was a child, he innocently wished John's family and my original family could live together in a giant house. But he was only a small child then.

Message to the Future

CHAPTER TWENTY-SEVEN

The Funeral

We could not see the name you called;
We could not see the hand that beckoned afar;
The wound in our hearts concealed, maybe in time will heal;
But ohhh!, the hurt will remain;
It all was so sudden, the shock so severe,
We thought a bright, promising future was near.
The ones who have lost you can only tell,
Of the heartache of parting and saying "farewell"

—Unknown Author

I sat in the funeral home staring at Justin's body. It looked darker than I'd ever seen it. I sat there thinking, *He is going to open his eyes, sit up, give me that Justin smile and say, "I'm alright Mom."* I kept looking, waiting and hoping; it was possible. Lazarus was raised from the dead. I read in the news someone woke up in their casket... The more I looked, the more I realized, I was looking at a shell. His spirit made him my son. His Spirit was gone. I wanted to crawl inside myself and get really small.

I felt movement. I looked up amazed to see, Mrs. Lyonns, Justin's cousin Paul, Uncle Kerry and several other people come into the wake. I stood up, hugged Mrs. Lyonns and thanked her for coming.

The funeral: 9-11-93

I was surprised to see the limousines were all white; I had only seen black at funerals. I guess it had been hard on Mike finding Justin's body and reliving those moments. He had arranged for a closed casket. Alarms when off in my head; I felt I was being robbed of a last opportunity. I insisted on an open casket because I wanted to see him one last time. I sat on the pew with the casket before me. The choir of older men sang, "How Can I Say Good-bye." Pastor Tim said words and a prayer. Then, like tall giants, my three brothers walked to the podium. Nick and Joe stood beside Loren as he delivered the eulogy:

> You entered our lives with the brilliance of a star being born in the heavens. With a blaze of glory, your life started. The glow of your light blazing a trail through life; filling our world with hopes and dreams of brilliance. Sometimes fading, but never far from sight and always appearing when the sky darkest. But just as a journey begins, it too, must end.

Sometimes sooner, sometimes later, never knowing which of these is greater. As a star has passed from our heavenly sight, within our hearts his light burns eternally bright.

As I viewed the body of my nephew, reality set in. I realized that I would never see his shining eyes, or hear his voice, or see his smiling face. In the midst of my grieving I found that I have something that not even death could take from me and that is the memory of a beautiful spirit. I began to dwell on that spirit that once dwelled in that earthly temple. A giving and forgiving spirit.

It is said that when Jesus Christ returns, we will have to give an account of our lives and someone may be asked to stand for my nephew. On that day, I pledge that I will stand for him as he stood for so many during his life, bringing comfort and joy to all who crossed his path.

I ask God in His infinite wisdom if he would return the soul of my nephew back into his peaceful kingdom. Gone, but never forgotten: Justin Mark-Adam Smith Lyonns.

They sat down. The funeral home director presented me with a large Bible with his name emblazoned on it. Then the pall-bearers came and lined up in front of the casket. They started carrying him out!!! I wasn't ready to see him go. My mind was screaming, *It's too soon. I'll never see him again!!!! OHHHHH, OHHHHHH, OHHHHH ... I can't just let him go.* I began to say out loud what I was thinking. In a broken voice, I yelled, "I loved you Justin! I love you now. I wanted you to LIVE! Live! Live!" I was thinking of all I wanted for him. But it would never be.

Somehow, I ended up across the aisle from where I had been sitting. Mike held me tenderly and said, "Let's sit down."

Through my cries of pain, I heard a comforting voice keep repeating something. I listened. I heard the voice say, "He is living. Mary Lou he is living."

I looked up. It was my friend Lorraine. She repeated it. "Mary Lou he is

living, " I swallowed, took staccato breaths and tried to settle myself. I sat to regain my composure; everyone left the church.

My family didn't understand my choice to cremate Justin. They tried to talk me out of it. Angela had asked to be cremated but Mother wouldn't hear of it. I could and would make this choice.

As I got into the limo, I caught a glimpse of Justin's half-brother. I remembered Justin saying, "Jamala is my girl. I take her riding around with me when I go places. I only knew his sister and brother from photos. I bent down, gave him a hug and said, "Be good. Do well in school. Justin loved you." I saw tears in Mrs. Lyonns' stoic eyes as we drove off.

Message to the Future

Everyone left Florida except Mother. During the time Mother was still with us, GiGi called to tell me, "John called me and said you hadn't cared much about Justin when you went out of town on business trips and left Justin alone. I know John needed someone to talk to so I listened to him." I defended myself saying that I had never left Justin without making provisions for him to be with someone, but he begged me not to make him stay with other people. I started having neighbors watch out for him. I did it because Justin was the same age I was when I was left in charge of all of you. It was uncomfortable, but we survived. But... Justin was alone ... My voice trailed off. I squeaked out, "I was wrong..." I handed the phone to Mother.

Since I wasn't talking to anyone, Mother said she would return home too. My heart hurt but I couldn't talk. Mike knew I was in pain. He offered to pay her to stay. She stayed a little longer but had to eventually go back to work.

Mike had to return to work too. The Lamm family was concerned about leaving me alone. Several family members showed unselfish compassion when they adjusted their schedules and made the long drive to our house every day to ensure I was never alone. Their presence probably kept me from acting on the real anguish I felt inside.

Message to the Future

Message to the Future

Part III

Message to the Future

Message to the Future

CHAPTER TWENTY-EIGHT

One for Sorrow

> One for Sorrow, Two for joy,
> Three for girl, Four for boy,
> Five for silver, Six for gold,
> Seven for secret never to be told
>
> —Mother Goose

My thoughts remained focused on why Justin killed himself. I started looking for answers before the funeral. From the telephone records, I determined Justin spoke with Darlene just before he called me at work. I called Darlene to find out if she had any hints of his desperation. She wasn't at the dorm but she returned the call and I immediately asked, "Did you think of anything you would like to share with me from your last conversations with Justin?"

"We argued a lot, but that was pretty much normal."

"Had he been calling you a lot and was he yelling and screaming when he called?"

"He called a lot, but he did not yell and scream."

Mrs. Tanner was wrong. In a relieved tone I said, "I didn't think so because I heard him on the phone sometimes and he seemed quiet. Was he upset about anything?"

"Not that I know of."

Then I asked the hopeful question, wishing for a remnant of my son. "Are you pregnant?"

"No, I thought I was; but no."

I paused in the conversation as well as mentally and emotionally releasing the last hope I had for some living version of him. In what I hoped was a controlled voice, I continued, "Was he concerned about coming back to Florida?"

"No, he seemed to want to go back. He was looking forward to it."

"I knew he was a little nervous about school. Did he say he had any concerns about school?"

"No. He talked about getting a 4.0 average."

"Did he say anything about his father?"

She quickly responded, "He L-O-V-E-D his father."

"I know." Silence followed. I repeated, "I know he loved his dad."

"I filled out a form to go with Justin to visit his dad, but time ran out and I wasn't able to go."

"I know. I saw the form."

"Did he tell you not to go to the football games?"

"No, he didn't know I was going. I decided at the last minute."

"I understand you two broke up."

"Yes, but we were still real close. We still kept in contact. But once I left Toledo, it was just different."

"That's normal. I tried to explain things to Justin along those lines." Then I poured my heart out, "I tried to keep Justin with me, but he wanted to go to Toledo to be with his dad. I didn't want him in that environment. It just so happened that by the time I had enough of his behavior, and allowed him to go stay with his grandmother, his dad was incarcerated. I wanted him to come back, but he would have to repeat the grade and graduate a year later."

Immediately after the rush of information, I regretted it, thinking, *she probably doesn't even care.*

"Justin didn't really care about finishing school, but I wanted it for him, so I would take him to school and pick him up from school."

"I know; and I'm very grateful to you for that." I paused a long time then asked, "Are you coming to the funeral?"

"I want to come, but my parents don't think it's a good idea."

"I can send a copy of the eulogy."

She asked, "Do you have the correct address?"

The police had returned his letters to me so I replied, "Yes. If you need anything, let me know. I'm thankful you called."

After the funeral, a counselor from Justin's Florida high school called. She said, "I read Justin's obituary in the paper and wanted to call. He came to see me when he returned to Florida."

I asked, "Did he discuss any problems with you, or mention his grandmother's accusation about him taking money?"

"We didn't discuss any problems. We talked about school and his girlfriend. He was upbeat and happy."

I replied, "That's what I saw also."

She went on to say, "Justin was always sweet and I enjoyed talking to him when he was a student here and also the last time we spoke. He seemed different, more together and mature."

"Thank you."

"I'm very sorry I don't know more."

I recalled Mrs. Lyonns saying, "Justin told John he felt so bad he could kill himself."

At that time, I had not thought to ask why he said it. I called to find out.

I first asked, "Justin had some artwork he made, would you send that to me?"

She hesitated a long time, "John has to have something of his to remember him."

When I asked about Justin's statement to her about killing himself, she hesitated a long time, finally she said, "I'm not sure why he said it."

At that point, I knew they had shut down. Whatever

they knew, I would never know. I also knew I couldn't and didn't trust them to be truthful.

I really don't know how we concluded the conversation. I'm sure it was done courteously.

I returned a family bible that Justin had. My note said, "I've been holding onto this for Justin. But you originally gave it to John and it rightfully belongs to him. He might want it now under the circumstances."

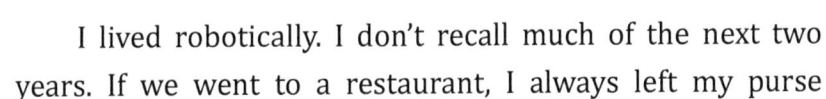

I lived robotically. I don't recall much of the next two years. If we went to a restaurant, I always left my purse behind, unless Mike reminded me to get it.

I had lost someone of great value, I guess my mind manifested that to mean I should lose something of value every day. I don't know. I just know I wanted to be Ms. Haversham in *Great Expectations*—I wanted time to stop—but no one understood.

My brother-in-law suggested grief counseling. My mother suggested Survivors of Suicide (SOS). They helped. With the SOS group—for the first time I sensed someone *really* understood how I felt losing a child to suicide. I attended several sessions. But I wanted to keep what I had left of Justin to myself; I wasn't ready to share him with anyone. I began to intuit this was a life journey so I had to find a way to move on from this helpful group. I would learn many things about myself; see the grace of the Universe, learn and realize that I would never understand many things.

Two months after his death, November 18th, I received a letter from Isabelle. It was dated October 19, 1993, and read:

> Dear Mary Lou,
>
> I had to wait until the rage inside of me subsided but the anger and pain are still there. It is that which I feel compelled to address to you.
>
> Many questions about Justin's death remain with me. Most of all I hope they will remain with you for a long time to come. You see, you were right; you weren't a good mother. You were too selfish and self-centered to care about the needs and wants of your child. You have always only cared about what you wanted and needed and even as a little child, Justin interfered in that. Well, now you don't have to worry about that anymore.
>
> He needed to know that you loved him, cared about him and accepted him unconditionally. Yes, he was a troubled child, constantly searching for attention and unconditional love, something he so desperately wanted from you. But he was always a thorn in your side to remind you of his dad and to prevent you from achieving your "professional goals."

Well, there is nothing to bind you with John now and nothing to stand in your way of achieving all that you want. However, I want you to know that I believe that you use people to attain what you want. John may not have lived the life that you wanted him to, but he financially provided for you and your family. I know he supplied the money for your mother to be able to buy the house on Summit Street and to enable Angela to go to school. Yes, even though he ended up in prison, one thing was sure, he loved his son and at least Justin knew that. John was able to accept him unconditionally, I cannot say the same for you.

The fact that you would not allow his body to come back to Toledo tells me one thing. You haven't changed. You're still just as immature, selfish and self-centered. The fact that you had his body cremated also has placed doubts in many of our minds about the nature of his death.

You can tell us anything but we will never truly know. We do know that he and your husband did not get along and that you and Justin still were not communicating well. He wrote and told his dad that much. So, you see, we don't know if his death was a suicide or if he was killed/murdered and it was made to look like he took his life. We'll never know because you destroyed the evidence. Did you have something to cover up? Whatever happened, I hope you are happy now and I hope Justin's ashes will bring you many years of contentment as you struggle with the pain and loss also.

Now that I've had my say, I feel somewhat relieved but your inconsiderate behaviors will never be forgotten.

Isabelle

P.S. You need not respond to my letter, your response must be to God and your own conscience.

I took responsibility.

The letter caused the intended pain. I imagine it was written on John's behalf. I knew the Lyonnses stuck together no matter what but I was surprised Isabelle would write such a letter. She was an educated woman, at least ten years older than John; I thought she was more compassionate.

I thought back to when she had the idea to have all her nieces and nephews for a week. She and John pleaded to have Justin be included. I shouldn't have caved because he returned with blisters on his bottom. She swore it happened in one day; she had been diligent. Of course John supported her.

Then I realized she could not possibly understand, she'd never given birth to a child. She had never struggled to raise a child. She didn't know what it felt like to hold a feverish child during the night and pray for the fever to subside, or pray that you keep your sight, health and strength, so that you could help your child grow or to keep watch that his shoes never got too tight so he didn't end up with bad or scarred feet. She had not worried that he never had to fight in some senseless war, nor had she had to struggle trying to establish a lifelong foundation of spirituality, strength, work ethic and intellect. She had not actively worked to expose him to varied positive experiences. She must not have known about the early weekend mornings dedicated to tap dancing or karate lessons; or about evenings working on homework. She had not tried to assist in protecting him from physical and emotional dangers so he could live to be a positive contributing member of our world.

It was clear John had fed her half-truths and even though she was an educated woman, that clan mentality had her act upon the half-truths. While John had provided for his child and me that first year, he never paid a dime of child support. The house was signed over to me because John got the deed from some drug person. It was given to me by John to try to make up for the many things awry in our marriage. My sister borrowed money from him but repaid every cent when her financial aid package came. Maybe Isabelle wasn't aware that I left that marriage with what *I* worked for. John kept his valuables in his parent's name or at their home. I didn't see Justin as a troubled child. At thirteen, he started surprising behavior but I believed we would move past that and he would settle back down.

She was correct in one thing, I could not get away from my vision of a better life to see through his eyes. I had always struggled with the notion that when working, time away from your child didn't matter as much as quality time with them. I didn't believe it but I knew I had to work and making it in a professional career was better for him and me. Yet, I didn't understand him when I should have and did not respond appropriately when I could have. Yes, I took responsibility. His death should have been prevented.

More Revelations:

My days were consumed traversing a torrid tunnel of regrets. Still in pursuit of understanding Justin's pain, I called the hospital psychology department counselor in Toledo and asked for Justin's file. To my surprise, Justin had told the doctor that he would get his parents back together one day! It is hard to believe that seven years after the divorce and even more years of separation, Justin dreamed of re-uniting his dad and me. He never got over our divorce!

Maybe he thought I would be like one of his aunts who reunited with her husband after a long separation. Maybe he misinterpreted my efforts to remain cordial with his dad for his sake as a sign that I would one day reunite with him. Maybe his dad told him there was hope and encouraged him to believe we would reconcile.

Confession-like, Mike divulged, "If Justin could have held out a little longer, I think things would have been all right. Just before he returned to Florida, I talked to Pastor Tim and Bobby about working with Justin and me. I realized that to have a real family, and to make you happy, Justin and I had to have a sincere, friendly co-existence."

I didn't respond. It was good to hear but Justin was gone. There was nothing to be said or done.

Someone from Toledo told me about Justin's last visit to John. Reportedly, John greeted Justin by punching him very, very hard in his chest as soon as he walked into the prison visiting room. His comment was, "I heard you've been disrespecting my mother." I imagined any words that followed were very unpleasant. Maybe that was what Mrs. Lyonns meant when she said Justin said he felt like killing himself? I also heard that when John heard his son was dead, he fainted. It reminded me of the time when John was being an awful husband, I told him he destroyed everything beautiful in his life. He cried.

My brother, Loren, told me Justin had stayed behind after the wedding reception trying to be helpful by cleaning up the rental hall. He joined them at the breakfast place but everyone was leaving when he arrived. He was furious. He had been left out. Loren said he offered to stay with him while he ate, but he said, "No" and heatedly drove away screeching the tires as he left.

I had not known about the situation, because the next morning he didn't show any sign of the hurt and disappointment he displayed the night before and no one mentioned it.

For some reason, I kept thinking about Joe asking me why I didn't take Justin with me on a shopping trip. So, on December 10, 1994, I called Joe to ask if I had missed something. He told me, "After you left the room, Justin said, 'Did you see that? She came in the room and didn't even speak to me.'" Joe immediately followed, "I told him you spoke to everyone in general, but he didn't think you paid attention to him. He was upset that you didn't ask him to go shopping."

"When I used to take him shopping with us he was bored and didn't want to go."

I encouraged him to continue, "Is there anything else?"

"It started a long time ago, when his dad went to prison. He was crushed. Then it was just the two of you. You and Justin went places together, did things together and everything was based around the two of you. When you left him alone, he was afraid. He felt like you two weren't friends anymore. The people next door were watching but he was scared. His dad was not there for him and you were not there. He called and told me he felt bad. Then Mike started coming around and he felt that you didn't want to be with him, you wanted to be with Mike. He called me and told me he felt like killing himself, but he made me swear not to tell anyone."

I felt more heartbroken as I listened. Joe knew. He knew for years and never told me.

He spoke politely and sincerely but I could sense anger. I encouraged him to continue. He sounded hurt as he disclosed, "When Mike bought him that jogging suit for Christmas; he was very happy. He really liked it and I thought things would get better. You know, he really hated Mike for a long time. He thought Mike took you away from him. He was disappointed at your wedding reception because he thought he should have sat at the wedding table with you and Mike. It didn't matter that he sat with the rest of the family. He thought he should be with you."

Then in a distant voice he said, "He gave lots of clues. He was just waiting for someone to show he was as important and could get as much time as he gave. He wanted everyone to show him love. He wanted to be included in things."

I said, "I made a point of trying to include him. He went everywhere we went."

Joe responded, "He wanted you to do things with him that he liked to do, like you used to play video games, watch TV, go bowling. You know he l-o-v-e-d to bowl."

I replied, "I tried to take him to do things with just the

two of us."

Joe countered, "He wanted you all to do things together. He thought Mike took you, then the three of you away from what he wanted to do. If you had continued doing things with him that he liked to do, it would have been better.

He didn't want to leave Florida to live with his grandmother. He told me you didn't have time for him. You sent him away. You put him aside for Mike."

I tried not to interrupt, I just wanted to gather as much information as I could. But at that I protested, "But that is what he said he wanted to do!"

Joe plopped his thoughts down, "I know. But that is not what he *really* wanted. Mother and I got into a big argument about that. I wanted to call and tell you, but Mother told me not to. She said you have a family; your own life. When she told me that, I yelled at her, "Justin IS her life."

I mentally applauded his wisdom and quietly asked, "Why didn't you tell me?"

He sadly repeated, "Mother told me not to."

Still seeking, I queried, "Did anything happen there to cause him to want to take his life."

Joe offered more information, about boys who were jealous of him. They wanted to fight him before he left because he had told the truth about something. It was something I didn't know ... it was an insight to an occurrence, but it was a small piece of the puzzle.

Through a lump in my throat I calmly asked, "Oh, is

there something else?"

Joe commented, "He always cried after he talked to his dad. He didn't like seeing him in prison. He thought his dad would always take care of him."

I inquired, "Did he say anything about the Lyonnses?"

Joe remarked, "He didn't talk much about them, but he said his grandmother didn't like him. He felt everyone in the family was against him and none of them really treated him like they loved him or liked him. He thought they treated him differently. His cousins, Paul and Randy could take any car the Lyonns family had when they wanted it, but Justin couldn't use a car for pleasure unless it was mine or Mom's. They were not treating him fairly. Justin said no one would go with him to his counseling sessions. He felt left out. When he had a problem or he did something wrong, everyone jumped on him. Everyone in both families yelled at him. No one sat down to try to talk him through his problems."

I knew Joe made Justin fill his Buick with gas each time he used it, even if it was empty when he got it. While he could have gone to the counseling sessions with Justin, at 21 he was not mature enough to step up.

I asked, "Did he say anything about taking money?"

Joe's voice changed. It sounded like he had discovered a missing puzzle piece. "I wondered where he got so much money. Justin had gotten accustomed to his dad giving him money, so when that got cut off, he didn't know how to adapt. He didn't know what to do. I saw him hang around a guy who had a bad reputation. He was a drug dealer. I asked him if he was involved with drugs. He said no, he didn't want to get into that. I kept asking him what was happening and he finally told me that when he didn't have any money, he would sell some of his dad's stuff to the dealer. He was not selling drugs. He would pawn his dad's saxophone, telephone or whatever. If he didn't find anything to pawn, he would steal."

Joe continued by opining, "Justin thought Mom's not around anymore. Dad's in prison. The family is against me ... But he helped everyone. He talked with everyone about their problems. He did what he was told to do and what he could for his grandmother. He helped me. He helped GiGi. He helped Mother ... he talked to everyone about any problem or tried to assist us. He did a lot of good things without ever mentioning his problems, even though he knew he had them. Darlene was all he had."

"Didn't he know that I loved him?"

Joe plowed on, "Justin said, 'Mom doesn't love me anymore, we don't go to the movies, play video games, ride go-carts or anything anymore. It used to be just me and her. No one wants me around. Everyone is leaving me out.' He wanted to go to the club to celebrate Nick's wedding but we said he was too young. He said he would sit outside; he just wanted to be around me."

Joe paused, his voice broke as he confessed, "I was so wrapped up in my girlfriend, and my problems that I wasn't there. At Nick's rehearsal dinner, he looked me straight in the eye and said, 'Joe, you are the closest one to me in the family but you're not my best friend anymore.' I told him, 'I love you man. I've been having a lot of problems. I love you.' But Justin didn't respond."

There was a pause then Joe hoarsely cried, "I know what it's like. I've felt that way before, but Nick was there for me. He was there to point out my problems and help me resolve them. Justin had no one to talk to. Everybody needs someone to talk to, or you start to think crazy thoughts. You need God when you feel you don't have anyone or you lean toward being bad, mad and frustrated. I never want to stand by and let that happen again to anyone else that I love or care about. It's my fault. I didn't take my experience and help him."

Compassionately I said, "Please don't blame yourself."

Angrily, Joe replied, "After his death, I told Justin's Uncle Karl that I wanted to speak to John. I wanted to tell him about himself and I wanted to tell you all of this too, but the rest of our family stopped me. Nick told me to wait because you might not know how to handle it. Everyone was concerned and Mom asked me not call."

His voice softened and, with conviction, he stated, "I will not intentionally put myself in a position that I can't be around for my son. John provided well for Justin. He sold drugs to provide for him, but then he was taken away from him when Justin really needed him."

I covered the phone to stifle the escaping sobs. I sighed deeply then changed the subject to inquire about his family.

He told me of the many health and relationship problems he had. Playing my "big sister" role, I tried to comfort him as best I could without displaying my own pain.

It was clear, what he told me that day might have helped two years earlier. I was glad he shared his thoughts with me. I was disappointed and sad that he had remained silent about something so serious. I wondered if mother knew the full extent of Justin's sadness when she talked him into staying in Toledo? So many mistakes ... We all were responsible; there were no innocents.

The truck smelled of death. Mike wanted to sell it. I wanted to hold on to it and any tiny connection to him, no matter how morbid it seemed. For many months I felt like I struggled with a 500-pound wrestler sitting on me, and I was left with just enough air to stay alive. I turned the same thoughts over and over in my mind. It was a daily mental war weighing the positives and negatives of my decisions and their impact on his life.

My grief counselor told me she thought suicide was an act of revenge. I didn't think that was correct in this case. He loved me. When she told me to read a book about the possible non-existence of God, I knew she couldn't help me.

Someone in SOS tried to be helpful by offering that he might have been depressed or mentally ill. I refused to label him mentally ill in posterity. Someone else offered it might have been drugs. There were no drugs in his system. He was sane and drug free when he was alive; he would remain so after death. I would not accept any rationale or blameless route. I didn't deserve any comfort; no avenue of reconciliation. All I was left with was a crumbled piece of paper I found in the trash can after the investigators left. The note left me with more questions than answers—except one: life was just too damn hard.

I took a long hard painful look at what I had provided my child. It started with me, after all I gave birth to him:

In trying to escape poverty and provide for us, I ran as hard and fast as I could toward a better life. I just hiked up my skirt, threw Justin on my back and went full force. I made choices that had my child separated from me at crucial points of his development. I do not regret making an escape from an impoverished life. I was sure I could create better circumstances than those I experienced. I believe with a little more support I could have been more successful. Success—an outcome that could only exist with my son alive—able to enjoy life.

I ruminated over the areas that led to the failure. It was hard to capture a specific thing I did wrong because life is so big and dynamic, yet I started where I knew less than optimal choices were made.

I had Justin out of wedlock. I had only completed one year of college. We were too young for the responsibility of being good parents; I was too young. I chose the wrong mate. Our values were unaligned. He was unfaithful. He became a drug dealer. It's near impossible to be a full father, or mother, if you can't be around to guide through those little moments.

My dad tried to tell me not to exacerbate the situation by making the mistake of getting married. I didn't listen to him or my mother. While their circumstances were different, they had not married and I suffered for it. I wouldn't do that to my precious child. Yet, my choices led to a worse outcome.

I had worked hard to cultivate open communication between the two of us. I thought I had succeeded. He told me lots of things, including the fact that he had contemplated suicide. But I didn't really hear him and I certainly didn't believe him. I believed statistics were on my side; he didn't fit the profile for suicide. I thought it was a rough patch and we would move forward to better times. I always believed he would have a full life. I could only see a promising future if I could just get him to choose to work for it. I'd not been good at understanding unstated and unshown feelings. I should have seen and understood. The marriage and the stable life I envisioned for us seemed bad to him. In many ways, I felt I had pursued a fake "good life." I had worked so hard to make things better and now my son was destroyed along the way. Much of what I worked for seemed meaningless without my son. Ultimately I was sure choosing to not pursue better living conditions was not an option I would or should have chosen.

During those days when I sat alone, sometimes I could "hear" a voice say, "I made a mistake, Mom."

I couldn't believe the voice I was hearing. It was so gentle and so unreachable. It didn't help. I couldn't tell if it was him or me wanting it to be him. My mind had difficulty holding on to the fact that there would be no more little moments. I could not look forward to hearing his voice on the phone, watch him walk down the driveway to the car, dance, travel to new and interesting places, eat a meal together, attend a concert together, or have his presence light up the room when he walked in the door. I missed his carefreeness and the jovialness he had before we moved to Florida. I will *always* miss his smile.

At first, I asked, "Why?" But in time I knew why in the all-consuming dull empty pain that caused my heart to hurt in knowing. He died at seventeen without knowing how to tie a necktie. Mike had tied one for him and he only partially undid it for the next use. I could not teach him how to be a man. I could only share what I hoped to have him become. Yet, many women had raised respectable men alone. I failed. I only wanted to protect him as best I could. In my effort to protect him, I had failed to see, to understand. I thought Mike would be a good model but negative influences had Justin reject him. I wish I had been wiser. In the final analysis, feeling unsupported, or valued or loved enough likely led to his death—just not getting enough of what he wanted and needed.

Message to the Future

AFTERWORD

Myself

As I walked by myself, And talked to myself,
Myself said unto me:
"Look to thyself, Take care of thyself,
For nobody cares for thee"

I answered myself, And said to myself
In the selfsame repartee:
"Look to thyself, Or not look to thyself,
the selfsame thing will be."

—Mother Goose

Mike gently encouraged me to return to work. He reasoned, "It'll keep your mind busy. It's good for you to interact with people. It'll get you out of the house into the fresh air and sunshine." I thought, *He just doesn't want to come home to another corpse to deal with.* Lonely and trying hard to function, I went back to work. My boss chastised me for taking so much time off. I fell into autopilot doing what was required for my daughter, husband, employer, family and friends. I was always tired and if I spoke, my comment was preceded and punctuated with a sigh.

Someone at work asked me if I wanted to become a Wicken. I asked if he meant a witch. He said all witches are not bad. Shocked and saddened, I declined. Two years later on a day before Labor Day, the company downsized and I was laid off work for the first time in my illustrious career. Maybe it was coincidental, but I wondered if my cold-blooded boss chose that date to increase my pain, then I thought, *not even he would be that heartless*. My mind exploded with screams, shouting and thrashing around while I sat quietly consuming it all, until I was exhausted. I started feeling I needed a chance to really grieve the loss of my son. I wanted to escape.

I often retreated to the silence of his room. I lay across his bed looking out the window like we used to do and listened in wonderment at the whippoorwill. Lightning broke the branch of the tree where the owl used to sit. The owl doesn't visit the tree anymore. In the spring, I listened for the whippoorwill to sing his distinctive song. I remembered Justin liked to tease me and had recently chortled, "Don't get too feisty, I might make you a grandmother."

To which I replied, "Not yet, I'm still too young!"

Those yesterdays are long gone. I stored the backgammon, checker, scrabble, yatzhee and Othello games we once routinely played.

It was only in reviewing my diary that I realized I had

chuckled that night, before he took his life. But it was because he didn't want to take money for running the errand and I knew he needed some money. His accusation didn't register because I would never laugh and would never have laughed about *anyone* taking their life.

I asked family to continue to pray for Justin and was miffed when they wanted to pray for me instead. I struggled desperately. If music was playing somewhere, I didn't listen. I mentally blocked it out. I committed myself to so much pain that my heart hurt and my head had strange sensations. It all became so uncomfortable that I was sure I would die unless I *decided* to live. My sister-in-law, Cynthia Royel, gave me a reason to live my best life. She wanted me to live my life in its fullness for my daughter's sake. She was right. She deserved the same best efforts I'd made with Justin. At first, I didn't know how to act on the decision. I had embraced sorrow so deeply, I didn't know the way out. I had begun to look at the world darkly; everything seemed negative. So, I took little steps each day, little commitments to myself that I kept, until I started to feel better.

It's been many years now. As the years unfolded, my cordial, courteous, quiet grief led to acceptance of the fact he is gone forever. I went from feeling misplaced in the world to depression before exploding into anger. My feelings constantly cycled between lonely depression, anger, fear that I never was, should have been or could be a good mother. If I walked past our beautiful, dining room table, I thought of taking a knife and marring it. I didn't act on it though. Overtime, I took up drinking wine. At times, usually in social settings that Mike gently pulled me into, I drank more than the doctor recommended one glass. That too had negative effects. I had never cussed. I started cussing at Mike. He bore the brunt of everything, yet miraculously, in some fashion, our marriage remained intact. I finally realized I needed help when during an argument I banged a tea kettle on the stove grates so hard the grate broke. That frightened me, so I spoke to another counselor. He listened, recommended a book, but had no real answers.

For years I didn't, couldn't, wouldn't release the pain because that was all that kept me tied to him. Now, I have to accept my humanness, understand that I made mistakes and forgive myself for any and all contributions I made to Justin's decision. It is the only way I can choose to live. But as a mother—the burden is heavy on me.

I have to forgive Mike for any part he played because he was doing his best. I have to forgive my mother for her part and just wanting a good life for me. I have to forgive the Lyonnses for being who and what they showed themselves to be. I even have to forgive John for being and doing what he thought served him best. But in the end, it gets back to I have to forgive myself.

Over time I developed a constant prayer to the Universe:

Dear Lord, I don't know how Your kingdom works.

Message to the Future

I don't know the details of what happens after death, but I pray that You take my son with You and allow him to grow in Your love, knowledge, understanding and strength.

Please let him be at peace and find the love, kindness and acceptance he sought on this earth. Heavenly Father I am told You are compassionate. I know my son took his life, but I pray You will let Justin in Your kingdom. And, forgive me for my trespasses. Amen.

I still hope that all who knew Justin will become more loving, compassionate and understanding as they remember his life and his death. Some mistakes can't be rectified. Sometimes they can only be learned from. This painful outcome is now a dark patch in the tapestry of my life.

Free will—our lives and existence on this earth are shaped with choices. I am continually faced with choices as my journey through life continues. I pray for insight. I pray for wisdom and strength; I pray I make good choices from here on.

Message to the Future

AUTHOR'S NOTE

This memoir is my recollection of events. I've related them to the best of my knowledge. I may have changed the names of individuals and places, I may have changed some identifying characteristics and details such as physical properties, occupations and places of residence. The conversations are not necessarily word for word transcripts. Rather they are retold in a manner that elicits the essence of the feelings and meanings of what was said. In all instances, the essence of the dialogue is accurate.

This story is offered in hopes it will help someone make decisions that allow them to navigate this world better.

If something portrayed or conveyed does not resonate with any reader, that message may not be meant for you.

In that case, discard it without further thought.

CPSIA information can be obtained
at www.ICGtesting.com
Printed in the USA
BVHW091339060522
636308BV00014B/685